Flower of the Winds

DOROTHY KEDDINGTON

SKYBIRD PUBLISHERS

Novels by Dorothy Keddington

Jayhawk
Return to Red Castle
Shadow Song

Note: All characters in this book are fictional, and any resemblance to persons living or dead is purely coincidental.

First printing December 1989

Skybird Publishing
9025 Chablis Circle
Sandy, Utah 84092

Grateful acknowledgment is given to the following for their kind and generous contributions to the research of this book:

To My Oregon Friends:

Nancy & Carl Hopkins, Tillamook
Barbara & Bob Watkins, Cape Meares
Dr. Hugh B. Wood, Oceanside
Fraynie Gedney, Tigard
Perry & Sharon Reeder, Tillamook
Don & Helen Cushing, Depoe Bay
Dr. Charles Miller, Oregon State University
The Officers & Crewmen of the U.S. Coast Guard, Tillamook Bay Station

To Those at Home:

Charlotte Colley, partner & friend
Mike & the Children
Patricia M. Keddington
Bethany Chaffin
Lt. Col. Edmund E. Hansen
Carol Warburton
Gerry & Janet Graves
Colleen Jensen
Doris Platt
John Watson
James R. Reynolds

Special Thanks To:

Former Ambassador Romuald Spasowski & his lovely wife Wanda
Michael & Lena Filshtinsky
Roger E. Turczynski
Robert Rozhdestvensky, for his poetry
Galina Vishnevskaya, author of *Galina: A Russian Story*

Loving Tribute is given
to the Memory of Walter Hatch
who asked me to write a book about Oregon. . .

for the Roseman

and

his little princess

priskazka
(prologue)

TWO TWENTY-FIVE p.m. and there was still no word as to the whereabouts of Dr. Nikolai Petrovsky and his assistant, Sergei Alexandrov.

Yelena Ivanova straightened a jumble of loose notes on the professor's desk, returned three stray paperclips to the drawer and brushed a smattering of eraser crumbs into the wastepaper basket. Dr. Petrovsky's able secretary was not ready to admit that something had gone wrong. To do so would be an admission that she had made a mistake, and Yelena was not willing to accept that. Not yet. There was still time. The small private jet was scheduled to leave Corvallis at three, and this early in the afternoon, the drive to the airport should take no more than fifteen minutes. Yes, there was still time. Their lateness could be the result of something quite innocent—car trouble or an unexpected delay at the Marine Science Center in Newport. Any moment now, one of those irritating Americans would probably call to assure her that Sergei and the professor were on their way.

Yelena closed the office door, then reached into her leather handbag for a pack of cigarettes. Her slender white hands were steady as she put the long filter-tip to her mouth and flicked the lighter. The slogan touted by the brand brought a cynical smile to her lips. "You've come a long way, baby." Typically capitalistic, she thought, and yet in many ways the words were true. She had come a long way since the days when she had been a struggling student in ill-fitting clothes. Excellent grades and a proficiency in languages had earned her a scholarship to Moscow University. Good looks and raw determination had done the rest. At the age of twenty-five, Yelena had been accepted as a translator for *Novosti Press Agency*, the publishing arm of the KGB. Now, at thirty-six, she enjoyed the privilege of travel and luxuries her parents could never imagine, let alone experience. She would never go back to her old life—living in a dingy, communal apartment, standing in line to use a common toilet, subsisting on cabbage soup and coarse black bread.

Yelena savagely stubbed the end of her cigarette in an ashtray and paced the small office. No one at the Soviet Consulate in San Francisco could question her handling of this assignment. She had kept Dr. Petrovsky under strict surveillance since their arrival at Oregon State University. Listening devices had been hidden in the professor's apartment and his office on campus. A voice-activated tape recorder was under the front seat of the car the Soviets were leasing from the University. In addition, there were weekly surveillance reports submitted by Dr. Petrovsky's assistant. Sergei Andreievich Alexandrov was prompt and his reports carefully worded. Sometimes a little too carefully worded, Yelena thought, but then, this was Sergei's first time out of the Soviet Union and he was young—barely thirty. It was understandable, perhaps even forgivable that his efforts were sometimes ambiguous. To be asked to inform on a colleague, especially one as widely respected and prestigious as Nikolai Petrovsky, was not an easy task. Still, every privilege had its price.

Yelena had watched Sergei Andreievich with interest during the six weeks since their arrival. As far as she could determine, the potentially dangerous exposure to capitalism had not corrupted him. Sergei was amiable enough with his colleagues and his brilliance in oceanographic research often earned the Americans' praise, but something about him always remained aloof and apart. That aloofness both irritated and intrigued Yelena Ivanova. Her instincts told her he was aware of her as a woman, yet Sergei had never displayed anything more than the casual warmth one would expect of a business associate. She knew, of course, that he was planning to be married soon after he returned to Leningrad, but that didn't hinder most men from enjoying their pleasures. Why should Sergei Andreievich be any different? It might be he feared and respected her position of authority. Or perhaps he was too inexperienced to recognize the subtle invitation in her eyes. More than once, she had kept Sergei longer than necessary at their weekly meetings, but nothing had come of it. Just last week she had asked him to have dinner at her apartment—an invitation he politely refused.

Yelena prided herself on her ability to read a man's motives and desires, yet this man eluded her. She admired the fierce dedication Sergei had for his work. She enjoyed his smile and the occasional flash of humor that lit his dark eyes, but it wasn't enough. Yelena wanted to see passion in those eyes—for her.

Perhaps that's why she'd told him. Sergei would have learned about the professor's imminent arrest soon enough, but she wanted to shock him out of his polite indifference, as well as let him know of her personal approval for his services. It might be her only chance.

Yelena's nervous pacing ceased and a soft smile played about her lips as she remembered the previous afternoon. Sergei had stopped by the office to inform her that he and the professor would be driving to Newport the following morning to meet with the crew of a research vessel.

"You haven't forgotten Dr. Petrovsky's lecture for the seminar in San Francisco?" she reminded him. "The plane leaves at 3:00."

"I haven't forgotten. We should be back some time after lunch—no later than two."

He wasn't even looking at her. Just sorting through a stack of mail. Yelena's gaze shifted from Sergei's hands to his broad shoulders and muscular body. In his American-made jeans and loose sweatshirt, he could almost pass for one of the students at the University. Yet, there was something about his deep-set eyes and the Slavic molding of his jaw and cheekbones that was uniquely Russian. Watching him, Yelena found her palms were moist and felt a sensual warmth growing inside her.

Sergei was turning to go, with nothing more than a casual good-bye, when she had stopped him short with, "See that you're back in time. I wouldn't want you to miss the little surprise we have planned for the professor."

Sergei had paused in the doorway. "Surprise?"

Yelena had given him one of her warmest smiles, softening the stilted words. "You are to be congratulated, Sergei Andreievich. Thanks in part to your excellent services, another enemy of the people will no longer be a threat."

The shock on his face was genuine. Yelena noticed with satisfaction that his knuckles were white as he gripped the door knob. There was no indifference now. When he didn't speak, she had risen and gone to him.

"You would find out about the professor's arrest soon, but I wanted to let you know myself—to give you my thanks, Seriozha." The affectionate nickname slipped out unnoticed as Yelena put a hand on his chest. She could feel the tautness of his muscles through the soft fabric.

"When is this to happen?" he asked, looking her full in the face for the first time.

"Tomorrow afternoon. Dr. Petrovsky will not arrive at the seminar," she told him, aware that her voice was a husky whisper. "Instead, he will be taken directly to the Consulate, then back to Moscow."

"I see."

Under her palm, Yelena had felt Sergei's deeply-drawn breath. "I know that Nikolai is your friend. It is unfortunate that a man of his position has allowed himself to become corrupted. Still, I also know that you understand."

"Yes," he had answered, covering her hand for a brief moment. "I understand."

Three twenty-five p.m. The small jet left Corvallis for San Francisco minus its scheduled passengers. Yelena Ivanova watched it gain altitude and bank away from the west where a heavy band of gray clouds was gathering. In seconds, the plane had turned south, into the blue. The rising wind cooled her cheeks and muffled the conversation of three men standing nearby. The small snatches drifting her way filled Yelena with a sweeping sense of failure.

". . . the Coast Guard in Newport?"

"Nothing."

". . . the police?"

"Not yet."

"Has there been a report on the vehicle?"

"Rusak and Smirnov are searching for it."

Yelena cast a final glance at the departing plane, now just a silver speck in the distance. One blink and it was gone. Like everything I've worked for, she thought, getting into a waiting car with three officers of the KGB.

"Before we drive to Newport, I want to see their apartment. I assume you have the keys?" Colonel Grigor Markevich spoke calmly, but his gray eyes were threatening as the storm clouds building in the west.

"Yes, Comrade Colonel."

"Good. It will give us a place to talk. And perhaps Comrade Ivanova, you will be able to explain to us exactly what has happened."

Yelena nodded and stared unseeing out the window as they drove away. Why? Sergei Andreievich, she questioned silently. You said you understood. . . .

Chapter 1

"I must go down to the seas again,
to the lonely seas and the sky. . . ."

John Masefield

DREAMS AND REALITY met and merged as I drove down the narrow wooded lane leading to Winwood Cottage. A west wind blowing off the ocean promised a stormy afternoon and by the time I parked my car in the covered carport beside the house, a soft rain was beginning to fall. I got out of the car and stood for a moment, breathing in the heady mixture of salt tang and sweet rain. Grandpa Hugh always loved the west wind, despite the storms which usually followed in its wake. In the soughing of the pines, I could almost hear his gruff voice telling me, "Keep your eyes peeled, Cassie-girl! You never can tell what a west wind'll blow your way."

Blinking back the tears, I shut the car door and slowly approached the house. The thimbleberry bush growing near the drive was tangled and untamed as ever. I walked past without pausing to pick any of its velvety red berries. Coming around the side of the house, my sleeve brushed against an overhanging cluster of hydrangeas, releasing a shower of pale blue stars on the wet grass. Out of habit, I stopped and stared at the uninhibited sweep of ocean and sky in front of Winwood Cottage. To the north, white mist blurred the rugged cliffs and forested headland of Cape Meares; to the south, the massive, wave-worn monoliths known as Three Arch Rocks rose out of the ocean. Today, I felt no surge of elation at the view. Instead, the somber sky and troubled seas were nothing more than a reflection of my own mood.

I turned my back on the ocean to gaze at the house. In my mind, I could see a tall man coming out on the wooden porch to meet me. His carriage was erect, his shoulders straight, the white hair a little thinner now, but still wavy. Set deeply in a raw-boned face, my grandfather's eyes were bluer than the sea on a sunny day.

I blinked and started forward, but only an empty porch and sightless windows stared back at me. More tears blurred my vision as I unlocked the door and stepped inside. Nothing had changed, yet the house felt as empty as if it had been stripped of all its furnishings. Closed curtains and pulled blinds drained the living room of color, leaving it a tired gray, and the air had a musty smell. Until this moment, I never realized there could be pain instead of gladness in the fulfillment of a dream.

For years, I'd harbored the dream of someday owning a home like my grandfather's on the Oregon coast. At times, the dream seemed elusive and out of reach, like the mist which hovers around the cliffs and coves on a stormy day. Other times, it could be as tangible as sunlight and the touch of warm sand. Warm or elusive, sunlight or mist, the dream was a part of me.

Occasionally, common sense inserted the reminder that even a "dream home" couldn't be as wonderful as Winwood Cottage. And when I was in the mood to be practical, I didn't mind conceding that as long as I had a place where I could wander the beach, explore tide pools and paint the many moods of the ocean, it really wouldn't matter what the house was like. But when practicality was impossible, and it frequently was, my mind persisted in seeing a rustic, gray-frame house on a forested hillside overlooking the sea.

Since childhood, I have watched sunsets, storms and the endless fascination of the waves from its windows. My senses have delighted in the color and fragrance of its gardens, where dazzling fuchsias and azaleas bloom alongside common daisies and nasturtiums. On summer nights, I have lain awake listening to the muffled music of the waves and the sigh of sea breezes through tall shore pines, hemlock and cedars. And whenever I take those worn wooden steps down the hillside to the beach, I know there will be some discovery or adventure waiting for me. It might be a ship on the horizon, a single shell or a pocket full of agates. More than once, I have found adventure just sitting on the smooth sand gazing out to sea, dreaming dreams as fragile as sea-foam. . . .

Now the dream was mine. But at a price I never wanted to pay.

I strode across the hardwood floor and pulled back the drapes, trying to ease the tight ache in my chest with some deep breaths. As I opened the window, the rain-fresh breeze blew a postcard off the old pine bookcase. I bent to pick it up and recognized my own handwriting on the back.

> Dear Grandpa Hugh,
>   Your letter was just what I needed to get me through a rough week. Now that my masters' art project is finished, I feel almost human. Spending July with you at the cottage will be heaven, so get ready for the smell of turpentine and oil paints! Until then, say hello to Gulliver and the ocean for me.
>   Love, Cassandra

I placed the postcard back on the bookcase, slowly sat down in my grandfather's favorite chair and buried my face in my hands.

It would have been an easy thing to let the rain and gray silence of the house feed my melancholy. Instead, I forced myself to unload the car before the storm grew worse. After half a dozen trips carrying in luggage, food and boxes of art supplies, the tight ache in my chest was completely gone—replaced by a sharp stitch in my side. I dumped the last box of canvas on a table in the upstairs storeroom and glanced about. The room was on the small side, but its light walls and dormer windows would be ideal for an artist's studio. My mind removed the dust and years' accumulation of boxes to see the finished product. Grandpa Hugh would approve, I thought with a smile, and went to work, finding an unexpected source of comfort in simple chores—dusting the furniture, moving boxes, just touching the things my grandfather had touched and loved for so long.

I was in the kitchen, nibbling a few Wheat Thins and trying to decide whether cream of mushroom or chicken noodle soup would be my fate for dinner, when a loud knock rattled the silence. I gave my heart a few seconds to calm down, then lifted the curtains near the back door, curious to see who had come out on such a stormy day. One look at the plump little woman standing outside and I let the curtains fall back, knowing the moment I said hello to my grandfather's nearest neighbor I would be saying good-bye to my quiet afternoon.

Living on a secluded stretch of coastline with no more than a dozen close neighbors might prove a social hindrance for most people, but not Muriel Davis. Grandpa Hugh had been fond of saying that no one died, was born, got married or dared get sick without her knowledge.

I unlocked the door with a sigh, wishing my arrival could have escaped her all-knowing eye a little longer.

"Hello, Mrs. Davis. How — ?"

"I heard your car a while back and thought you might enjoy some of my clam chowder for your dinner tonight. How've you been, Cassie?"

"Fine thanks, but —"

"I brought along a few brownies, too, in case you fancy 'em."

The woman bustled past me to set the pot of chowder on the stove and a plastic container on the counter. Following at her heels was a large gray cat with gold eyes.

"Gulliver! I wondered where you were."

"I've been feeding him over at my place since your grandpa passed away," Mrs. Davis said as I bent down to pick up the cat. "The poor thing's been so lonesome. George said I ought to take him to the animal shelter, but then I found out you were coming back to the cottage and figured he'd be good company."

"He certainly will. And the chowder smells wonderful, but I really don't need so much —"

"From the looks of you, I should've brought more! My laws, Cassie, I swear you're even thinner than the last time I saw you. Hugh told me you were nearly working yourself to death at that fancy eastern art school. I'm all for higher education, mind you—my boy Howard is only three quarters away from his B.S. My Lois would have graduated if she hadn't met Norman first, and let me tell you, there's been more than once I wished she hadn't!—but I still say there's no point ruining your health."

I laughed and assured her, "I'm fine. In fact, I've gained a couple of —"

"You know, looking at you is almost like seeing your grandmother. Margaret's hair was a darker brown—yours has such a pretty gold shine to it—but she had the same green eyes and fair skin. I don't know if I'd have called her beautiful, exactly, but folks sure sat up and took notice whenever Maggie Winwood came into a room. She even had that little cleft in her chin. Strange, isn't it?"

I wasn't sure if she were referring to my chin or my resemblance to my grandmother. Before I could ask, Mrs. Davis sighed and went on, "Well, I hear you're finally engaged. I'll bet your mother's relieved. When I was a girl, twenty-five was considered an old maid, but nowadays age doesn't seem to count for much. Who's the lucky man? Is he from around here?"

I drew a long breath and decided to ignore her pointed reference to my age. "His name is Kevin Barlow and his family's from Beaverton, so I doubt you know them."

"One thing's certain," she declared, taking my left hand in hers. "Your young man must be doing pretty well for himself if the size of that diamond is any indication."

I glanced at the showy solitaire, still not used to seeing the ring on my finger. "Kevin's very generous."

"Let's hope he stays that way, dear. When do I get to meet him?"

"Not for a while. Kevin's in New York on a business trip."

She gave me a sympathetic cluck of her tongue. "I'll bet you're just pining away. Have you set a date for the wedding? I want to hear all about it."

"Well, we're talking about the end of September, but we still —"

"That's real sensible. I'm glad you're not going to have one of those long engagements. No point in having too much time for second thoughts, I always say." She gave my hand a pat and headed for the door. "I've got some jello and a loaf of pumpernickel in the car. Be right back!"

I smiled and sat down on a kitchen chair with Gulliver in my lap. The cat's purrs filled the silence with contented rumbling until Mrs. Davis scuttled in moments later, depositing a loaf of bread on the counter and a bowl of red jello in the refrigerator.

"My laws, that rain is still coming down!" she pronounced, removing her scarf and shaking raindrops from apricot-tinted hair. Her raincoat joined the scarf across the back of a chair as she glanced out the window with a frown. "The weather report this morning said we'd get a few scattered showers. I should've known that meant we'd get hit with a downpour!" She sat down, removed her rain-speckled glasses and proceeded to dry them with a corner of her blouse.

I looked at the brightly-colored polyester straining across her bosom and covered a smile. The garish gold and purple paisley reminded me of some psychedelic amoebas having an orgy.

"You never can count on those fancy computer reports," Mrs. Davis went on, warming to the subject. "Now it used to be, if I wanted to know what the weather was going to be, I'd just come up here and ask your grandpa. Nine times out of ten, he was right on the button!" She sighed and pushed the glasses back on her nose. "It's a real shame about Hugh. There wasn't a soul who knew him that didn't respect your grandfather. I'll bet there were a few noses out of joint when the Winwoods found out he left the cottage to you. 'Course, I wasn't a bit surprised myself. You always were Hugh's favorite. Did your folks tell you I was the one who found him?"

Gulliver nudged my hand, begging for another scratch behind the ears, but my fingers remained motionless.

"No . . . they didn't."

"He was sitting out front in that old lawn chair—you know the white one he was so partial to. The mailman'd left a package for him that day, so I thought I'd save Hugh the trouble of going all the way down to the road to get it. At first, I thought maybe he'd just dozed off. He had his chair facing the ocean the way he always did, and the afternoon sun was warm. There was scarcely a breeze, as I recall. Then I saw his face. . . ." Her voice trailed off in another sigh. "Somehow, I think that's the way Hugh would have wanted it—no fuss and no hospitals. His passing was real peaceful, Cassie dear."

I nodded and stared out the window where raindrops ran in watery ribbons down the glass.

"Well, I've got a few minutes to spare. I'll be glad to help you do some cleaning up."

"I don't want to keep you —"

"Nonsense! Many hands make light work, I always say."

I dumped Gulliver off my lap as she went to the cupboards under the sink and grabbed a can of cleanser. "I appreciate the offer, Mrs. Davis, but I really don't feel like starting anything else this afternoon. Maybe another time."

The woman glanced at me, then reluctantly returned the cleanser to its shelf. "I just thought things might be sort of hard for you, being here alone and all."

"Right now, I need a little time to myself. I hope you understand."

"Of course I do." The woman's light blue eyes misted over as she pulled me close. "But if you need anything or get feeling too lonesome, just give me a call. I was telling George just the other day that I was real worried about you staying here all by yourself."

"You don't need to worry. I'll be fine." I lifted her coat and scarf off the chair and held them out to her. "Thanks again for the dinner. I was just wondering what to fix when you came."

"You're welcome, dear. You know how much your grandfather always enjoyed my chowder."

"Yes, I know. . . ." I opened the back door and glanced outside, determined not to start crying again. "The rain doesn't seem so heavy now."

"Well, I'll be going then." Mrs. Davis tied the scarf under her plump chin with the order, "Don't forget to let me know when your young man gets back. I'm real anxious to meet him."

"I won't forget."

"And you be sure to call me if there's anything you need."

"I'll be sure to call."

Halfway out the door she stopped and turned back with an apologetic frown. "I forgot Gulliver's cat food. Maybe I'd better run over to my place and get it."

I stepped outside, hoping she would follow. "Don't worry about it. I'll just open a can of tuna fish. I can get him some cat food tomorrow."

"Well, if you're sure —"

There's no need to make another trip out in the rain."

Mrs. Davis patted my cheek as she trotted past. "Speaking of being out in the rain, you better hurry inside, Cassie, or you'll get soaked!"

I didn't need further encouragement to do exactly that.

By early evening the wind had calmed and the rain was little more than a soft drizzle. I built a driftwood fire in the fireplace, made myself a cup of hot cocoa, then settled down on the couch with a Helen MacInnes novel I'd been wanting to read for months. My original plan to do some painting after dinner had been interrupted by no less than half a dozen phone calls. First, it was my mother wanting to know how I was feeling and if the house was warm enough. Next, Mrs. Davis called to ask if the clam chowder tasted all right because she was sure she'd forgotten to add salt. Ignoring my glowing praise, she launched into telling me about the time three years before when the minister had asked her to make a huge pot of chowder for a church social and she'd forgotten to add salt. After listening to a lengthy discourse of her suffering and humiliation over the incident, I finally managed to convince her the soup I'd had for dinner was perfection itself.

Not five minutes later, my sister Charlotte called from Tillamook to let me know she and her family were leaving on their vacation in the morning and would I mind driving over once or twice during the week to check on their house. The receiver was still warm when Kevin's mother phoned to tell me our engagement proofs had arrived and she'd found the perfect place for our reception.

After hanging up, I glared at the telephone, daring it to ring again. Naturally, it didn't and fool that I am, I went back to my painting. Three minutes later, Kevin called.

"I've been trying to get through to you for the past hour," he complained good-naturedly. "Who've you been talking to, your boyfriend?"

I laughed and decided I might as well clean my brushes and try again in the morning.

Now, after reading the same paragraph for the fourth time, I realized I wasn't making any better progress with the novel than I had with my painting. Tossing the book aside, I got off the couch and faced the front windows. Brooding gray clouds huddled on the horizon, blocking almost all light from the setting sun. I watched the waves toss and break against the sleeping form of "The Old Man of the Sea," my grandfather's name for Three Arch Rocks, and found myself hoping all seamen had found safe harbor for the night. And I would be wise to postpone my walk on the beach until morning.

I left the window to search the bookshelves, but nothing appealed to my restless mood. From his corner of the couch, Gulliver watched my pacing with imperturbable gold eyes.

Everywhere I looked, there were bittersweet reminders of my grandfather—the blue glass float we'd found after a fierce winter storm, a weathered piece of cedar driftwood, a jar filled with polished agates—our bounty from countless beachcombing expeditions. Hanging over the fireplace was one of my first seascapes, a gift for Grandpa Hugh's seventieth birthday. In the years following, I'd offered to replace it with paintings I felt were much better, but he always refused. Now, staring at the canvas, I suddenly realized I could pack it up, flaws and all, and store the picture in the attic. I turned away from the fireplace with a sigh, knowing I wasn't ready to make changes yet, any more than I was ready to face the emptiness of my grandfather's room.

Hoping some music would improve my mood, I flipped through the stack of albums in the cabinet of Grandpa's old Magnavox record player. Sibelius was too somber; I was already depressed enough. And Rachmaninoff was too passionate. I paused to examine a recording of Rimsky-Korsakov's "Scheherezade," then put the record on the turntable.

If I'd wanted to escape the memories, I never should have chosen "Scheherezade." Old feelings surfaced as the music transformed sounds to images of stormy evenings past, with my grandfather holding me close while wind and rain rattled the windows. Tonight, his presence filled this room and the bitter reality of his absence ached in my breast. All I had to do was close my eyes to hear his deep voice relating tales of Sinbad's exciting voyages across uncharted oceans. I especially loved the stories Grandpa Hugh made up about Sinbad and the beautiful young Princess. Instead of Scheherezade, the Princess' name was Cassandra, and of course, she looked exactly like me. As I listened to him, the cozy living room disappeared, and I would see the Princess Cassandra waiting on a twilight shore which vaguely resembled the beach below my grandfather's house. Whenever the sails of Sinbad's ship appeared on the horizon, I could be sure that romance and adventure were never far behind.

My grandfather never went into much detail about Sinbad's appearance, except to say he was handsome in a "rascally sort of way." In my own mind, I could see him very clearly. With his black hair and flashing eyes, his foreign, mysterious smile, there was more than a hint of danger about Sinbad, yet the Princess eagerly followed him into every escapade. My childish mind never questioned the sensibility of her devotion. Somehow, I understood that being with him was all that mattered. . . .

The dream faded along with the music, leaving me with a nameless longing—one which had nothing to do with grief over my grandfather's death. As I stared into the flames, the image of my fiance's face slipped into my thoughts. It shouldn't matter that Kevin wasn't mysterious or exciting like the Sinbad in my childhood fantasies. He was affectionate and dependable, and there wasn't anything he wouldn't do for me. What more could I want?

I straightened up with a guilty sigh, suddenly remembering how much Kevin had wanted me to go with him on his business trip. And yet, when I'd told him about my plans to stay at Winwood Cottage for a few weeks, he hadn't argued or tried to change my mind. Even though I knew he was disappointed, he said he understood.

Tonight on the phone, I'd heard some of that same disappointment in his voice. When he said he loved me, my response had been an automatic. "I love you, too." But after his whispered, "I miss you, Cass," something prevented me from answering the same. Instead, I'd told him lightly, "You'll be back in a week. The time will fly. You'll see."

Remembering his hurt silence only deepened the guilt I was feeling, yet I knew I would still choose to have this time alone at the cottage. Was it wrong not to miss him?

Shoving the uncomfortable question aside, I got off the couch and went to the hall closet for my windbreaker. Rain or no rain, I was going for a walk. Halfway to the door, the habit of years and my grandfather's stern reminders sent me back for a flashlight. I grabbed one off the closet shelf, slipped it into my pocket and left the house.

The gray dusk and light-falling rain made the wooden steps down the hillside a bigger challenge than usual. Twice, I had to clutch at vines and undergrowth to keep from slipping. The moment I reached the sand, I discovered wind and rain weren't the only deterrents to my plans for a walk. One look at the high water mark along the shore told me the tide was coming in. It wouldn't be long before the path around the point was completely underwater.

I faced the incoming tide with growing frustration. In the misty twilight, there was no horizon, only gray sky merging and melting into stormy gray sea. The air was filled with the roar of sea-thunder as great swells of dark water rose into curling waves which crashed and broke over the rocks. Tonight, something in me needed the sea's restless fury more than comfort and warmth. Turning away from the hillside steps, I shoved my hands into my pockets and struck out across the sand.

Chapter 2

MOVING TRAILS OF sea-foam bubbled and hissed against the barnacle-encrusted walls of the point as I walked by. A few yards ahead, three gulls were clustered around the remains of a crab. Farther down the beach, more gulls flirted with the tide in their search for food. I stepped around a snaking ribbon of seaweed and walked on. Despite the fading light, I found myself searching the wet sand for the shape of a shell, or perhaps an agate, even though my chances of finding anything were slim. As I walked, my frustrations faded like the faint horizon, and I gave myself up to the fascination of the sea. For now, this was all I needed—a salt-laden breeze, the mournful cry of gulls mingling with the roar of the surf and soft rain misting my face and hair. I smiled as a line of verse surfaced in my mind. Lord Byron was right. "There is a rapture on the lonely shore. . . ."

I paused to follow the flight of a gull as it left the haven of the cliffs to soar over the waves and suddenly found myself staring at a graceful white shape caught in the jagged teeth of some offshore rocks. For a startled moment, the gray dusk made me doubt what I was seeing. I wiped a damp strand of hair away from my face and climbed onto a large, humped rock for a better look. It was a boat—a small cabin cruiser. It couldn't have been trapped for too long or the Coast Guard would be on the scene. There didn't appear to be anyone on board. I bit down on my lower lip as the pounding force of a wave smashed against the boat's sides, sending plumes of spray high into the air. I knew I should go back to the house and call the Coast Guard, yet for some reason, I felt reluctant to leave. Seconds passed as I scanned the surrounding sea. There was no reason to wait. Even so, before climbing down from the rock, I paused for one last search of the foaming waves.

There! Not far beyond the breakers, I glimpsed a speck of orange and a man's head bobbing on the crest of a swell.

I yelled and waved my arms, but he couldn't see or hear me. What was worse, trapped as he was in the rolling swells and troughs, he probably couldn't see the shore. I tensed and caught my breath as the orange speck disappeared in a deep trough. Agonizing seconds dragged by before I spotted him again. He was still swimming, but the current was pulling him south, away from the beach, toward the cliffs.

"No! Over here! Over here!"

The wind and surf swallowed my cries, and I felt a sick helplessness rush over me. The next moment, some deeper instinct took over and I grabbed the flashlight out of my pocket. The strong white beam caught the swimmer head-on, and as the next wave carried him a few yards closer, I realized there were two people in the water. Yelling and waving the light, I willed them toward shore and felt a flooding surge of relief when the swimmers changed direction. They'd seen me!

If the men had been trying to fight an outgoing tide, they never would have stood a chance. Watching their weak strokes and flailing arms, I knew the cold water must be sapping their strength. My lips mouthed a silent prayer which ended in a startled cry as a dark wave rose and broke over them in a thundering wall of foam. When I found them again, one man was floating helplessly in the water, while the other struggled to save them both.

I dropped the flashlight and jumped off the rock. Tossing aside my windbreaker, I ran headlong into the surf. The force of an incoming wave nearly knocked me off my feet, and I fought to keep my balance as the shock of cold seawater rushed over me. Then I was swimming out to meet them.

I dived under a rising swell before it had a chance to break, then surfaced and glanced around. Only yards away, a bearded man bobbed on the sea's turbulent surface, while another man clutched his life jacket with one hand and reached out to me with the other. In the spray and foam of the next wave, I lost sight of that outstretched hand, and panic spurred my strokes. The next moment, our fingers met and clung.

"You're going to make it!" I yelled. "We're almost there!"

With the injured man between us, we fought our way through the breakers. Two more waves carried us into the shallows, and I struggled to my feet, feeling the full burden of the bearded man's weight. Broad through the chest and stockily built, he was about my height, no more than 5'7". His companion was taller and younger, though it was too dark now for me to see his face clearly. Between the two of us, we half-dragged, half-pulled the older man across the slick, onto dry sand. When I knew we were safe, my strength left me, and I fell to my knees, gasping and shivering from the cold.

I seriously doubted whether I had the strength to attempt mouth-to-mouth resuscitation, but the younger man was already removing his companion's life jacket and laying his head on the man's chest.

"Is he breathing?"

He looked up, nodded, then shuddered violently. The injured man was beginning to shiver as well.

"We can't stay here," I said through chattering teeth. "We've got to get around the point before the tide cuts us off. Can you carry him or do you want me to go for help?"

The man's features were little more than a gray blur, but something in the sudden tensing of his body reminded me of a wild animal when it scents danger.

"The tide," I repeated. "If we don't leave now, we'll be trapped!"

The desperation in my voice must have gotten through to him because the next moment he was on his feet, tossing aside his own life jacket and hoisting the bearded man over his shoulder. Without a word, he followed me across the sand.

The rain had stopped, but the night breeze blowing through my sodden clothes felt colder than the sea. Shivering, I pushed on through the gloom, ever aware of the labored breathing and heavy steps of the man behind me. We were nearly to the point when I remembered my windbreaker and the flashlight. Even if there were time to go back, it was too dark now to find them. Straight ahead, the rocky walls of the point loomed like a giant black shadow beside the darkening sea. As we approached, the heavy splash of waves lapping against the rocks confirmed my fears.

I glanced at the tall man and put a restraining hand on his arm. "You'd better wait here while I see how deep the water is."

Not waiting for his reply, I ventured into the sea once more. Ten steps out, an incoming wave soaked me past the knees, but the water was only calf-deep.

"It's not too deep yet!" I called over my shoulder, then waded back where the men were waiting. "We can still make it if we stay close to the rocks."

The younger man shifted the weight of his friend's body across his right shoulder and waded in after me. We were nearly around the jutting edge of the point when a "sneaker wave" unleashed its sudden fury on the rocks, drenching me breast deep and threatening to pull us under. The tall man shouted something that was drowned in the wave's wet thunder and quickly moved behind me, blocking my body with his. We clung like starfish to the rocks until the wave subsided, then plunged forward through the foam. As we headed toward shore, the man stayed close by my side, letting his body take the full force of the waves. Once, he stumbled and swayed and my arm went quickly around his waist. Not until we were out of the sea's grasp and staggering across dry sand did I release my hold.

"My home's on top of the cliff straight ahead," I told him, pointing to the dark hillside above the beach. "There's a path and some steps just beyond those rocks."

Thoughts of a warm fire and dry clothes quickened my pace. I must have climbed half a dozen steps before realizing the tall man had slumped to his knees below me, unable to carry his burden any farther. I scrambled down the wooden steps and knelt beside him, my emotions twisting at the harsh, ragged sound of his breathing.

"I'm sorry. I didn't mean to leave you."

The older man was leaning against a rock, moaning

something, but shivering so hard his words were unintelligible.

I draped one of his arms around my shoulders. "Try to stand. Please . . . I'll help you. It's not far now."

The tall man took his friend's other arm and stood up with a groan. One step at a time, we struggled up the steep slope, with the chill wind at our backs and the sea grumbling below us. Although the bearded man was conscious and trying his best to walk, his efforts were clumsy and uncoordinated. Danger signals of hypothermia flashed through my mind, but I kept my voice calm and encouraging. "You're doing fine. We're almost there."

At last we were out of the wind and into the shelter of the pines, with the lights of Winwood Cottage shining like a beacon through the trees. Their welcoming gleam seemed to give the men a much-needed boost of energy as we hurried up the lawn to the house.

Once inside, the younger man helped his friend to the couch while I rushed to add more wood to the fire. Urgency heightened by fear made me want to add ten logs instead of two and cover the men with a dozen quilts. *Take it slow. Just take it slow. Too much heat too soon can be as dangerous as the cold.* My grandfather's calm instructions seemed to come out of nowhere, overriding the fear, as I remembered the time I'd fallen overboard in a boating accident. Grandpa Hugh had carried me back to this house, stripped off my wet clothes and wrapped me in a flannel blanket, then prepared a steaming pot of peppermint tea. I took some steadying breaths and felt the panic ease away, replaced by calm certainty of what I needed to do.

The older man lay on the couch, his stocky frame convulsed in shudders. Blood trickled down one side of his face from an ugly gash on his temple, but at least it wasn't gushing.

"Start getting his clothes off," I told the man bending over him. "I'll be right back with some blankets and bandages."

I was searching the shelves of the medicine cabinet when I noticed my left hand was streaked a bright red. I stared at the blood in surprise, thinking it must have come from the injured man. But after washing my hands, I discovered my palm and several fingers were scored with fresh abrasions. It must have been barnacles, I thought, remembering that precarious moment at the point when we had clung to the rocks. At the time, I'd been aware of only two things—the rushing sea and the tall man's body shielding mine. Now, pain sent a stinging message to my consciousness. I dabbed a little antiseptic on the cuts and quickly wrapped some gauze around my palm.

There wasn't much else in the way of first-aid supplies. Taking what was left of the gauze, I grabbed the antiseptic, along with some adhesive bandages, then hurried from the room. The linen closet had plenty of blankets and towels. I snatched two of each off the shelves, then, without a moment's hesitation, opened the door to my grandfather's room. There was no time for sadness or even wistful memory. I slipped a blue bathrobe off its hanger, took some pajamas from a dresser drawer and left.

During my absence, the younger man had removed his friend's jacket, shoes and stockings. I set my supplies on the coffee table behind him as he struggled with the shirt buttons.

"I can manage the rest," I offered, touched by his shivering efforts. "You'd better get your own things off."

He hesitated, then reached for one of the bath towels. I sat down in his place and soon discovered my bandaged hand and sore fingers didn't make the task any easier. I was vaguely conscious of the tall man standing behind me, peeling off his soggy sweatshirt and Levis, but most of my attention was focused on his bearded friend. He was still shivering, but not as hard as before. The lines around his eyes and forehead, along with the salt and pepper beard, led me to guess he was in his mid to late sixties. In spite of the man's pallor and weakness, I felt an innate sense of dignity about him. He did his best to assist me as I helped him out of the shirt, but the simple act of lifting his arms seemed to exhaust what little strength he had. Taking one of the flannel blankets, I spread it over the top half of his body, removed his trousers, then covered him with the rest of the blanket.

"How are you feeling? Any warmer now?"

He nodded weakly, intelligent hazel eyes gazing into mine. "You are . . . very kind."

I smiled to hide my worry and tucked the flannel more closely about his shoulders. "That cut on your forehead has stopped bleeding, and I think the seawater has done a pretty good job of cleaning it. To be safe, though, I'd better use some antiseptic. It might sting a little."

He flinched only once as I cleansed the cut and wiped the blood off his face. The adhesive bandages did a fair job of holding the edges of the wound together, at least until a doctor could determine whether stitches might be necessary.

"There. How does that feel?"

"Much better. . . ." His eyes followed me as I gathered up the first-aid supplies and got stiffly to my feet.

"As soon as I've changed clothes, I'll make us all some hot tea," I told him. "I'm sure you're going to be fine, but that cut might need stitches. I'll be glad to call your doctor or the paramedics —"

"*Nyet!*"

I jumped at the deep-voiced command and jerked around to find Sinbad standing before me, naked except for the towel around his hips. My lips parted as I took in the breadth of his chest, the sinewy shoulders and arms which looked as if they could brandish a sword or climb the rigging of any ship. It didn't matter that his hair and eyes were dark brown instead of black. I knew him instantly. Danger glittered in those deep-set eyes, and there was a sense of mystery shadowing the strong bones of his face. For a lightning-swift moment, I felt an answering gleam of recognition in his eyes, then I glanced away and tried to find my voice.

"Wh — what did you say?"

"There must be no doctor. I will attend to him."

"You?" I took in the low, heavily-accented tones in a daze. It was even Sinbad's voice, the syllables deliciously slurred and foreign. I shivered and tried to gather the shreds of my common sense. "Are you a doctor?"

He shook his head and insisted, "There is no need for doctors. We are . . . much recovered. . . ." His voice trailed away as he swayed toward me.

Bandages and the bottle of antiseptic clattered on the floor as I reached out with both arms to steady him.

"No doctors," he mumbled against my shoulder. "Much

recovered . . ."

"You're not recovered! Please . . . you need to sit down."

His damp hair against my cheek smelled of the sea, and I was far too aware of his muscular body against mine as I helped him to my grandfather's chair near the fireplace.

He sank into the big armchair without resistance, but his husky voice was still adamant. "No doctors —"

I leaned over him, smoothing the dark, tangled hair from his forehead. "Shhh. We can decide what to do later. Right now, you need to rest."

One of his hands moved to cover mine, trapping my bandaged palm against the smooth planes of his cheek. Without warning it came again, the pull of unspoken attraction between us, as strong and irresistible as the tides of the sea. The feeling frightened me with its intensity, and I snatched my hand away.

"Did I hurt you?" he asked, glancing at my bandaged hand with concern.

"No . . . no, it's only some cuts from the stupid barnacles."

The hint of a smile lifted a corner of his mouth. "Stupid barnacles?" he repeated with that incredible accent.

I drew a shaky breath. "Yes . . . well, if you think you'll be all right for a few minutes, I'd better get out of these wet clothes." I plucked nervously at the front of my blouse, then cringed, realizing the damp, clinging fabric left little to the imagination. I bent down and gathered up the men's clothes, hoping to hide my embarrassment, if nothing else. "I'll — uh, take these things out to the laundry room. Your shoes can dry on the hearth." Holding the wet clothes in front of me, I added, "There's a robe and some pajamas on the couch. I don't know if anything'll fit, but at least they're dry."

Sinbad gave me a courteous nod and said something which sounded like, "Spa-se-ba," adding in English, "Thank you."

"You're welcome."

I backed away from those dark eyes, then turned and fled the room.

Chapter 3

UNANSWERED QUESTIONS teased and troubled my thoughts as I undressed in the upstairs bathroom. Sinbad . . . who was he? Where had he come from? And why had he been so insistent that I not call medical help for his friend? I draped my damp clothes over the bathtub, then gave my chilled skin a brisk rubdown with a towel, trying to insert some common sense into the matter. Just because the man was attractive and had an accent didn't mean he was shrouded in mystery or that his motives should be suspect. His behavior could have been triggered by trauma and exhaustion, nothing more.

Finding a rational explanation for my own behavior wasn't so simple. As much as I might want to, I couldn't dismiss that startling moment of inner recognition or pretend it hadn't happened. He had felt it, too.

I hurried back to my bedroom, stumbled into a clean pair of jeans, then pulled a soft cotten sweater over my head. Maybe trauma was having a different kind of effect on me. That, plus an active imagination. I sat down on the bed and picked up my hairbrush with a shaky sigh. Never listen to "Scheherezade," then go for a walk on the beach.

Not counting the time I spent tearing the cupboard apart searching for the jar of dried peppermint, it didn't take long to make the tea. On impulse, I added a few of Mrs. Davis' brownies to the tray, then headed for the living room.

Both men were seated on the couch, heads bent in deep discussion. When they saw me, their voices ceased too abruptly for the conversation to have been a casual one, and something in their wary glances made me feel like an intruder. It was all I could do to set the tray on the coffee table with a few minor tremors.

"Sorry to take so long. I hope you're feeling better."

"Much better." The bearded man's smile was warm, and I was relieved to see his skin no longer had such a pasty look. My grandfather's blue bathrobe was too long in the sleeves and length, but it wasn't a bad fit for his stocky frame. "And yourself?" he asked. "You are also recovered?"

"I'm fine," I said, thinking it must be nerves or my imagination again that was making me so jumpy.

The sight of Sinbad dressed in silky, wine-colored pajamas did nothing to calm my nerves or my imagination—especially with the top hanging unbuttoned against his tanned chest. All he needed was a dagger in his teeth and a scimitar at his side.

I glanced down and concentrated on pouring the tea, then handed the first cup to the older man. "Do you need some help or can you manage?"

"I can manage, thank you."

Sinbad took the second cup without comment, and for a few moments, none of us spoke. The way the men downed the hot tea and brownies made me wonder how long it had been since they'd eaten.

"Is very good," the bearded man told me.

"Please have more. I made plenty."

He thanked me and held out his cup. When I offered more to Sinbad, he shook his head and asked carefully, "The clothes . . . they belong to your husband?"

"No. My grandfather."

His dark eyes made a quick inspection of the adjacent dining room and hall. "And this grandfather—he is here?"

"My grandfather died almost a month ago."

"Ah. You are alone then."

The significance of his words sent an uneasy chill through me. I set my cup and saucer on the table with a jittery clank.

The older man turned to him, gentle rebuke in his voice.

"Where are your manners? This beautiful young woman saves us from the sea and all you can do is ask questions." Leaning toward me, he said softly, "I thank you for my life."

A feeling of calm replaced my uneasiness as I met his eyes. I was certain the man meant me no harm, yet I couldn't dismiss the feeling something was wrong. "What happened?" I asked. "How did your boat end up on the rocks?"

A swift look passed between them before the bearded man answered, "We had engine trouble and lost all power."

"Why didn't you call the Coast Guard? They could have towed you into Garibaldi . . . Good heavens, the Coast Guard! I forgot to call them and report the accident."

I jumped up from my chair. Before I could take two steps, Sinbad sprang from the couch, crossing the distance between us. The cup and saucer which he tossed carelessly on the table teetered on the edge, then toppled off as he grabbed my arm.

"No Coast Guard!"

"But I have to report —"

"There must be no Coast guard!"

If I hadn't seen the fear in his eyes, I would have been terrified. Even so, it took a few seconds to find my voice. "No doctors, and now, no Coast Guard. That doesn't make sense—unless you're in some kind of trouble."

He hesitated, softening his hold on my arm. "Our trouble does not involve you."

"I think it does. You're in my home, wearing my grandfather's pajamas, and—and now you want me to break the law by not reporting an accident!"

Confusion clouded his eyes as he struggled to find the logic in what I had said. I felt the heat rise in my cheeks and added indignantly, "And you've spilled tea all over the carpet!" as if that were all that mattered.

"Sergei, we have no right to accept the young lady's help and offer nothing in return—not even an explanation," the older man put in.

The man called Sergei answered him in a language I didn't understand, yet there was something distinctive about the clipped consonants and strange, backward-sounding phrases. I stared, wide-eyed, as the men argued back and forth, suddenly realizing what part of me must have known all along.

"You're Russian . . . aren't you?"

Sergei said nothing, but the tightening of his mouth gave silent affirmation to my words. When he released my arm, my knees nearly buckled under me.

"I think perhaps it is time we should make introductions," the older man inserted into the room's potent silence. "My name is Nikolai Matveyevich Petrovsky, and this handsome young fellow who spills tea on your carpet is Sergei Andreievich Alexandrov. I am professor of oceanography at Leningrad University, and Sergei is my assistant. During the month past, we have been studying with American scientists at your Oregon State University."

The combination of warmth and formality, not to mention the revelation of his introduction, left me speechless. I faced the Russian professor in a daze, then extended my hand.

"I . . . I'm happy to meet you, Dr. Petrovsky."

The man lifted my fingers to his lips in a courtly gesture. "I would be pleased if you would call me Nikolai."

It was difficult to resist his warmth and smile. "Nikolai," I agreed.

"And now, may we know your name?"

"Cassandra Graves."

"How lovely," Dr. Petrovsky responded. "And how fitting. Cassandra is Greek, is it not, meaning 'helper of men.'" He paused, and his expression grew serious. "I wish there were some way I could thank you for your help and kindness. Instead, I must ask for your silence. It is most vital you do not call Coast Guard regarding our accident with boat."

I met his intense look with quiet firmness. "I'm sorry, but I can't do that without knowing why."

Beside me, Sergei Alexandrov made a restless movement and spoke in Russian to the professor.

I turned to face him. "Look, you don't need to speak Russian. I already know you don't want to tell me anything."

"It is not a question of wanting or not wanting," Sergei explained in the tone one would use with a child. "There are times when knowledge can be very dangerous."

"And there are times when not knowing can be just as dangerous," I countered. "Now, if you'll excuse me, I'll get something to mop up that tea before it stains the carpet."

I half-expected him to stop me, but he didn't. Uneasy silence followed me into the kitchen where I grabbed some paper towels and a bottle of Windex. As I turned to leave, my gaze focused on the wall phone near the doorway, and I stopped short. There was no reason why I shouldn't call the Coast Guard right now. No reason besides the fact two Russians had asked me not to. I knew what Kevin would say. That I was impulsive and far too trusting. Calling the Coast Guard was the smart, sensible thing to do.

My mouth was dry, and there was a frantic little pulse pounding in my throat as I set the towels and Windex on the counter and carefully picked up the receiver. I stared at the numbered buttons, but all I could see was the fear in Sergei's dark eyes when he pleaded, "No Coast Guard!" The dial tone hummed in my ear as I remembered the quiet desperation in the professor's voice. "It is most vital you do not call Coast Guard. . . ."

My return was met with rigid silence.

I knelt down, sprayed some Windex on the stain, and scrubbed it furiously. "I didn't call them if that's what you're worried about."

Dr. Petrovsky's relief was expressed in a long sigh, and I didn't need to glance up to feel Sergei Alexandrov's dark-eyed gaze. I tossed the used towels into the fireplace, my heart pounding hard and fast, then sat down to face the two Russians.

It was Nikolai Petrovsky who finally broke the silence. The gravity of his voice held me motionless. "Tonight, Cassandra, you made a difficult decision. When you saw us in the water, you could have stayed safely on shore, leaving our fate to God and the waves. Instead, you risked danger to yourself in order to help us. Now, once again, you place yourself in risk by not calling Coast Guard." He paused to put a hand on the knee of the man beside him. "In this way, you are much like my friend, *Seriozha*. He, too, made a difficult decision, placing himself in great risk."

Sergei met his friend's eyes, gave a brief assenting nod, then looked toward the fire.

Satisfied, the professor folded his hands in his lap and turned back to me. "You have honored us with your trust. In return, we offer ours to you, although I fear you may find it an unwelcome burden." Dr. Petrovsky's keen hazel eyes assessed my reaction to his words, then he said calmly, "Yesterday, Sergei learned I was to be arrested by KGB."

For a wild moment, I felt as if I'd been dropped into the pages of the Helen MacInnes novel I'd been reading earlier. "Arrested? Why?"

He hesitated, then lifted his shoulders in a fatalistic shrug. "One does not always know why. It may be someone in Soviet Union envies my position, or perhaps I have come under suspicion because of my frequent association with Americans. The reason is of little importance. Once KGB identifies someone as security risk, it is *do svidaniya* — good-bye."

The calm finality in his voice was chilling, yet something in me found it difficult to accept what he was saying. "But you came here to work with our scientists. Why would the KGB want to arrest you for doing your job? I thought *glasnost* was supposed to change things like that."

"*Da*, there have been changes," he agreed. "And some are quite attractive on the surface. Forgive me if I sound like the skeptic, but after so many years . . . ." He sighed and shook his head. "To me, Mother Russia under communist system is like a tired old woman. New leaders come along to give her a fresh dusting of face powder and bright rouge. From a distance, she appears youthful, revived. But underneath —" Nikolai's voice lowered as he leaned toward me. "Underneath she is same tired old woman because the system has not changed. And KGB is vital part of communist system," he added grimly. "I will explain. When Sergei and I begin preparations for this research trip, I ask for my secretary, Pavel Perchonok, to accompany us. At first, I am told this is acceptable. Then, only days before we are to leave, I am informed Pavel has a heart problem which would make the trip most unwise, even dangerous to his health." Nikolai gestured expansively with his hands. "My superiors express great concern to me and make profuse apologies, but I am not to worry because University will kindly provide another secretary—Yelena Ivanova, a capable and attractive woman. Naturally, I must accept this arrangement or abandon my plans for working with American scientists. But inside I know that Yelena Ivanova is provided by KGB, not University."

I stared at him. "How did you know?"

Dr. Petrovsky's smile was cynical. "My dear Cassandra, for one to survive in Soviet Union, suspicion of everyone's motives becomes second nature. Besides, I know very well Pavel Perchonok is healthy as a horse. At least, he used to be," he amended with a sigh. "When I meet new secretary, my suspicions are further aroused. Ivanova is most pleasant and willing, but I am not talking to her five minutes before knowing oceanography is not her *spetsialnosti*. And her typing. . . ." Nikolai raised his eyes. "Does KGB think I am stupid donkey? I know from the first, Yelena is not secretary, but *stukach* — an informer."

Sergei Alexandrov spat out an angry Russian phrase, and I was startled to see the bitterness in his eyes.

The professor answered him softly. "That no longer matters, *Seriozha*. You know I understand."

The young Russian raked a hand through his thick brown hair. "It does matter!" he insisted. Then he glanced at me. "What Nikolai does not tell you is that Yelena Ivanova is not the only *stukach* hired by KGB."

My thoughts whirled at his implied admission. Sergei—a paid informer?

"A trip outside Soviet Union is a great privilege," Dr. Petrovsky went on to explain. "One that is given to a select few. There are many scientists, older and more experienced than Sergei, who would gladly inform on their own mothers for the chance to travel." Nikolai looked at the younger man without blame or reproval. "You are my friend as well as my colleague. It is natural for KGB to approach you. What happened was not your fault. If you had refused them, Yelena would never have confided in you, and I would be on a plane to *Moskva* this very moment."

I looked at Sergei in surprise. "Yelena told you about the

arrest? Wasn't she taking an awful risk?"

Sergei answered me with a careless shrug, but his expression was decidedly uncomfortable.

"A woman will often take risks when she wants a man," the professor said bluntly. "Ever since our arrival, I notice Ivanova is taking special interest in Sergei. What is your American expression? — 'making the moves' on him. Yelena was certain that Sergei would be flattered, that he would welcome an invitation to her bed. Naturally, were this to happen, it would increase her control over him and provide an excellent source of blackmail."

My glance slid to the man who was staring tight-lipped at the floor, a tinge of ruddy color staining his cheekbones. "I'm afraid I don't care much for this Yelena."

"Which is precisely *Seriozha's* problem," Nikolai agreed, spreading his hands. "But Yelena is his superior, and he must be careful never to reveal his true feelings. Yelena may have sensed Sergei's lack of interest, but she is not a woman who gives up easily. Even knowing that Sergei and his Natalya were to be married upon our return was no concern for her, only an added challenge. . ." He broke off and sent the younger man a swift look of apology. "Forgive me. I am a thoughtless fool."

Sergei shrugged away the man's words, but I had already seen the pain which filled his eyes.

Something twisted and tightened inside me. Why couldn't her name be Olga or Ludmilla? — something that suggested a plain, square-faced girl with a figure to match. Natalya conjured up visions of a classic beauty in a painting by Botticelli. The next moment the vision was shattered by the stark realization that Sergei Alexandrov would most likely never see his fiance again. The magnitude of his decision cut through me with painful clarity. Remain silent and allow the arrest of a friend, or risk everything— safety, position, loved ones, perhaps even his own life. . . .

My gaze shifted from Sergei's bowed head to the professor. "A few minutes ago, you told me I was like your friend because I had a difficult decision to make." I drew a deep breath and shook my head. "You honor me by saying so, but it isn't true. I don't think I could ever be that brave or unselfish. . . ."

Sergei straightened up, and the sudden light in his eyes sent warmth flooding into my face. I glanced down in confusion.

"No one knows what he will do until the moment of decision arrives," Nikolai said gently. "But remember this, Cassandra. If I did not feel trust for you, we would not be speaking so freely now."

Confidence in that trust led me to ask him, "What happened after you learned about the KGB's plans?"

Nikolai answered without hesitation. "This morning, Sergei and I drive to Newport for purpose of meeting with marine biologists there. The day promises to be a busy one because at three o'clock, I must take plane to address seminar in San Francisco. Then Sergei tells me if I get on the plane, I will not arrive at seminar. Instead, KGB will make arrest and take me to Consulate." His hazel eyes were direct. "Please understand, I have no wish to leave my country, to place family and friends in danger, but defection is now a choice I must consider." The professor leaned back against the cushions with a heavy sigh. "Did you know, Cassandra, the word 'defector' does not exist in Russian? Our language has but two words for those who leave the motherland— traitor and emigrant. To Soviet authorities, both words mean the same. So you see, for us there is no easy decision." He rested his hands in his lap with another sigh.

"Kolya and I will always love Russia," Sergei told me, fierce loyalty edging his voice. "But Russia and Soviet government are not the same. And so we make our decision. The motherland we will keep here —" He touched his left breast. "But Soviet Union we must leave . . . separate ourselves. . . ." He broke off in frustration. "It is difficult to express, to make one understand."

"No, not so difficult," I answered softly.

"Sometime after lunch, Sergei and I tell our colleagues we are returning to University," Nikolai went on. "But we do not return. Instead, we leave the car near Marine Science Center and walk to Coast Guard Station. There we intend to ask for political asylum, but when we arrive, men are leaving in a great hurry. A fishing boat is in trouble, and we are left not knowing when they will return." Anxiety tightened his voice. "Every minute increases our danger. I want only to disappear where KGB cannot find us. We know they can trace the car, and we have little money. Then I remember my friend, Dr. Harrison, who has fine boat in the marina. Considering the seriousness of our situation, we decide he will not mind if we borrow it for a few hours."

I stared at the two Russians. "You took his boat? How did you manage that without a key?"

"That would have been a problem," Nikolai agreed, "were it not for my friend's poor memory. Bill Harrison is a fine scientist, but he has, as we say in Russia — *dyr'avaya golova* — a holey head." The professor touched his own head and smiled. "He is very absent-minded. Last time we go fishing with him, Sergei notices that a spare key is taped under one of the seats. And so we make our escape."

"Where were you planning to go?"

"At first, it does not matter," the professor admitted frankly. "Then once we are out on open sea and thinking more clearly, I realize we must find someone in authority to help us—someone who will not turn us over to KGB," he added grimly. "Last time I visit this country, I met a man in Astoria who works for Customs and Immigration. Even though he was important person in your government, I found him to be honest and caring. This impressed me. The more I think of him, the stronger my feeling becomes that he can help us. And so we sail north. Unfortunately, the boat's engines interferred." A shudder shook the professor's stocky frame, and he sagged wearily against the couch.

I leaned back in my own chair, trying to take in everything they had told me. Dr. Petrovsky was right. Their trust was a burden, not unpleasant, as he described it, but one heavy with the weight of new knowledge and awareness. In recent years, political defectors had become a common item in the news. I'd felt passing sympathy for their plights, but their situations were far removed from the realm of my own experience. Life went on, with more wars and more tragedies filling the headlines, and the names of various defectors were soon forgotten. Now, looking at the two men across from me, I realized my feelings about defectors would never again be so detached and impersonal.

Sergei's deep brown eyes met mine, and I took a steadying

breath.

"I understand now why you didn't want me to call a doctor," I said, "but if you went to the Coast Guard in Newport, why don't you want me to call the station in Garibaldi?"

"In Newport, we had not yet stolen a boat and crashed it on the rocks," he answered candidly. "If we call Coast Guard, they will call Dr. Harrison at University to report accident with his boat. When University officials learn where we are, KGB will find out as well. Now is most dangerous time for Kolya. It is better—safer, if no one knows where he is until safety can be made sure."

And what of your own safety? I thought. Surely the danger must be as great, perhaps even greater.

I turned to the professor with new urgency. "What's your friend's name—the man in Astoria?"

"Miklos. Paul Miklos."

"I think you should call him right now. You're welcome to use my telephone."

Both men stared at me.

"It is enough you give us shelter and accept our words," Nikolai said, his voice faltering. "I cannot ask for more."

"You don't need to ask—I'm offering. Astoria is only a couple of hours' drive from here, but I think a phone call is probably the safest thing. The telephone's in the kitchen."

Relief eased the tight lines of worry on Nikolai's face as he reached out to clasp my hand, but his attempt to stand was short-lived.

"You must rest, Kolya," Sergei cautioned, as the professor sank weakly on the couch. "I will make the call."

"He's right. Please, lie down."

"All this fuss," Nikolai grumbled, waving away our concern. "I am fine — just a little tired."

"After what you've been through, you have every right to be tired." I picked up the flannel blanket he'd left at the end of the couch and shook out its folds. "Now lie down and put your feet up." I spread the blanket over him and threatened, "Unless you want me to call the paramedics, the Coast Guard and the entire U.S. Navy, you'd better not move off this couch! Understand?"

Dr. Petrovsky nodded, his eyes twinkling. "It is long time since I was bossed by a woman. I had forgotten how pleasant it can be."

I smiled and gave his hand a squeeze. "You just rest. We won't be long."

Walking through the dimly-lit dining room to the kitchen, I was very much aware of Sergei Alexandrov's tall presence by my side.

"What did Dr. Petrovsky mean—about it being a long time?" I asked, needing to fill the silence with simple words.

"Kolya's wife died five years ago. He has had much loneliness since then."

"Oh. My grandfather was a widower, too." I took the telephone directory from a kitchen drawer and chattered on. "You called him Kolya. What does that mean?"

Sergei leaned against the counter as I flipped through the pages of the directory. "Kolya is affectionate nickname for Nikolai, used by family and close friends."

I glanced up from the phone book. "Didn't he call you something else—I mean, a name other than Sergei?"

He nodded and answered in that low, musical voice, *"Seriozha."*

I wanted to say the name aloud, to test the sound of it on my lips, but resisted, afraid that doing so would introduce even more intimacy than I was already feeling. Suddenly, he seemed closer—so close, if I reached out my hand I could touch the tanned smoothness of his chest.

"What are you called by your friends?" he asked.

I swallowed. "Cassie — or Cass."

"The names do not suit you. They are much too plain." The curve of his mouth softened as he looked down at me. "In Russian, the nickname for Cassandra would be *Kasenya.*"

"Ka-sen —"

"Ka-sen-ya," he pronounced slowly, the name sounding like an endearment on his lips.

My breath caught in my throat, and I glanced down at the directory in confusion. "I've forgotten his name."

"Whose name?"

"The man in Astoria."

"Oh." It was Sergei's turn to look disconcerted. "Paul Miklos."

"It's long distance, so I'll have to get the number from the operator."

He watched with interest as I called information and wrote the telephone number on a pad of paper.

"Would you like to make the call?" I asked, offering him the receiver. "Just dial '1' before the number."

Sergei hesitated, then took the phone and punched in the numbers. A frown narrowed his brows as the seconds passed. "No one answers."

"He might be out for the evening. It's only a little past ten. We can try again later."

He nodded and hung up.

"How long has it been since you've eaten more than tea and brownies?" I asked, noticing the drawn look around his eyes and mouth.

"This morning. It does not matter."

"It does matter! No wonder Dr. Petrovsky's so weak. Since we have to wait before calling Astoria again, I have time to fix you some supper."

"We are causing you much trouble."

"It's no trouble. I've got tons of chowder, and there's a loaf of pumpernickel and some jello."

Sergei's expression was puzzled. "Tons of chowder?"

I laughed. "Well, not tons, but a lot—a large amount. I'm sure you'll both feel much better after you've had something to eat."

When he smiled, the brooding Tartar disappeared, replaced by a warm, much younger man. "It sounds good. *Ja golodny kak volk.*"

"What?"

He put a hand to his bare middle and translated, "I am hungry as a wolf!"

We laughed together, then fell silent almost the same moment as awareness began building in warm waves between us.

I turned away and opened the refrigerator, letting the cold air fan my flaming cheeks. "I — uh, it won't take long to heat the chowder. Maybe you'd better tell Dr. Petrovsky we weren't able to reach his friend."

Sergei mumbled something as he turned to go, then paused in the doorway. "Thank you," he said, adding in a husky tone, *"Kasenya. . . ."*

Both men did justice to Mrs. Davis' clam chowder, and they made sizable dents in the jello. Watching them, I couldn't help wondering what Mrs. Davis would think if she knew two runaway Russians were enjoying the food she had brought for me. A strange sense of unreality washed over me, and for a moment I could hardly believe it myself. Here I was, having a late-night supper with two Russian defectors as if it were the most natural thing in the world. And that was the strangest thing of all—that it should seem so natural. The crackling fire, the steaming chowder, Gulliver's contented purrs from the hearth, the two men wearing my grandfather's clothes. . . Grandpa Hugh would like them, I thought. I could almost see him and Nikolai sharing jokes and experiences over a chess game. And Sergei . . . Sinbad . . . The names entwined as my mind painted a canvas with summer skies, a sunlit sea and Sergei helping my grandfather haul in the day's catch. . . .

The canvas was erased by the professor's deep voice. I quickly glanced his way. "I'm sorry. What did you say?"

"I wish to thank you for an excellent meal." He smiled and patted his ample waistline. "The chowder was delicious."

I smiled in return, thinking I ought to give Mrs. Davis credit. Instead, I said simply, "I'm glad you enjoyed it," and stacked his dishes on the tray alongside Sergei's. "Maybe Paul Miklos is home by now. Would you like to give him another call?"

Nikolai glanced at the younger man. "Seriozha, if you would not mind? Rather than incite another lecture on my health, I think I will stay here."

"You are a wise man," he answered.

While Sergei placed the call, I rinsed the dishes off in the sink, trying not to appear overly anxious as the seconds stretched out.

"Still, no one is there," he said with a frustrated sigh.

"Give it a few more rings."

Finally, he shook his head and hung up the receiver.

"Well, we'll just have to try again in the morning," I said more cheerfully than I felt. "If he's still not home, we can call the Customs' Office—or even the FBI."

Sergei faced me with a frown. "Our staying here is imposition—perhaps even a danger for you."

"It's not an imposition, and as long as no one knows you're here, there's no danger. We both know Dr. Petrovsky isn't well enough to travel. Besides, where would you go?"

He had no answer for this, and I went on, trying to sound sensible and efficient. "My grandfather's room is just off the dining room. I think Dr. Petrovsky would be comfortable there. And there's another bedroom upstairs."

"Where do you sleep?"

"It doesn't matter. The couch is fine."

"The couch is fine for me, too."

"What?"

"I will sleep on the couch. It would be better if I am near Kolya."

"Oh . . . of course." I switched off the kitchen light and headed for the hall. "There are plenty of sheets and blankets in the linen closet. I'll get some to make up your bed."

Sergei followed me without a word, but the amused twist to his mouth said he knew exactly what I had been thinking.

When we returned with the bedding, Nikolai was sound asleep on the couch. With his bearded face relaxed in sleep, he seemed younger and more vulnerable.

"Poor Kolya," Sergei whispered, looking down at his friend. "All his life he has worked for Soviet State, given his brilliance and his energies. Now, abruptly, it is an end to all this. For him, Russia is now the past. . . ."

My gaze lifted to Sergei's face. "And for you?"

"For me, too," he answered bleakly.

Nikolai was half asleep as Sergei led him to my grandfather's room. The older man sank gratefully onto the bed as soon as I turned down the bedcovers, mumbled his thanks and was asleep once more.

Silence, solemn as a shroud, hung about us while I made up Sergei's bed on the couch. The young Russian sat in my grandfather's chair, staring into the dying flames. When I glanced at his face, my own sense of loss over Grandpa Hugh's death seemed a small thing. There was nothing I could say. No words of solace could ease what he must be feeling.

I smoothed a crease from his pillow, then straightened up. "Well, I guess I'll go to bed now. Good night."

Sergei didn't speak or look up, just gave the barest nod to acknowledge my words. I stood for a moment, aching inside as I watched him, then turned off the lamp and left him sitting alone by the fire.

Chapter 4

I LAY SLEEPLESS for a long while, mentally replaying the evening's incredible events. A hot shower had soothed and relaxed my body, but my mind refused to let go of all that had happened. Outside my bedroom window, I could hear the murmur of the sea, along with the pines' breathy whisper and the comfortable creak of cedar boughs, but even these couldn't calm my troubled thoughts. By now, the two Soviets must have been reported missing. Their American colleagues at Oregon State, not to mention Soviet officials, were probably in an uproar. What would happen if our government refused to grant them asylum? What if they were turned over to the KGB?

I turned over with a restless sigh and stared into the darkness. Tomorrow morning, Sergei Alexandrov and Nikolai Petrovsky would leave my life as suddenly as they had entered it. There was no point in worrying about anything beyond that. At least for tonight they were safe.

The thought brought little comfort. Were they safe? Sergei and the professor had been seen at the Coast Guard station in Newport. It was very likely that someone might remember seeing them at the marina as well. And their car. By this time, the authorities must have found it. But whose authorities . . . ours or theirs? I shivered and pulled the blankets closer.

Tomorrow morning, someone was bound to discover the boat. After that, it was only a matter of time before the Coast Guard produced the owner of the pleasure craft. It wouldn't take much effort or intelligence to connect a missing boat belonging to an OSU professor with two missing Russians visiting OSU. And when that happened, the search would begin almost at my front door. There was always an off chance the Coast Guard would presume the boat's passengers had drowned, especially since there was nothing to indicate any survivors had made it to shore.

I sat bolt upright in bed. Yes, there was! The men's life jackets had been left on the beach, along with my windbreaker and the flashlight. I put a hand to my breast, as if that could calm the fear pounding inside me. Maybe the tide had washed everything out to sea. But could I afford to take that chance? There was only one way to be sure—go down to the beach at first light and search.

The problem with that plan was I hadn't packed an alarm clock. One of my reasons for coming to the cottage was to relax and forget about the demands of the clock—to let the sun and moon and tides be my timepiece. I drew a determined breath and lay back down. I'd just have to set a mental alarm instead. Five-thirty ought to be early enough. Five-thirty. I repeated the numbers in my mind, afraid now to go to sleep for fear I wouldn't wake in time.

I needn't have worried. I woke promptly at midnight, again at one, then two-thirty. Frowning at the luminous face on my wristwatch, I set it on the night table and tossed back the covers. As long as I was awake, it wouldn't hurt to check on Dr. Petrovsky. Not bothering to put a robe over my satin nightshirt, I felt around for my slippers, then left the room.

The house was wrapped in soft black silence. I tiptoed down the stairs, avoiding the fifth step with its betraying creak, and cautiously approached the living room. Keeping to the outer edge, I moved quietly across the floor, not risking so much as a glance in the direction of the couch.

The door to my grandfather's room had been left slightly ajar. From within came the sound of Nikolai's deep breathing and some-thing else—a low, rumbling purr. Poking my head inside, I could barely make out Gulliver's round shape at the foot of the bed, where he'd slept when my grandfather was alive.

I smiled and tiptoed away, feeling comforted as well as reassured. The emptiness I'd experienced earlier in the day was gone. And somehow, Gulliver knew that, too.

Halfway across the living room, a low moan halted my steps. I backed away from the window's revealing outline, into the dark folds of the drapes and listened. Except for my pounding heart, all was still. Then, just when I'd gathered enough courage to move, the sound came again—a soft, tortured plea from the darkness.

There was nothing I could do to help him. I knew that. Yet, even as I turned to go, another restless moan drew my steps toward the couch instead.

The fire was a misshapen mass of chalky gray with only a few embers still glowing orange. Beyond its small radius of light, the room, the sofa and the man lying there were cloaked in darkness as soft and thick as fine black wool. I ventured a few steps closer, then froze as Sergei mumbled something in Russian. My rapid heartbeat slowed to a jerky thud when I realized he was only dreaming and talking in his sleep.

As I stood there, the darkness surrounding us diluted to a fuzzy gray, and I noticed a faint, milky glow from the windows. In seconds, the gray brightened to silver, then the clouds thinned and parted, revealing a waxing gibbous moon. Where only moments before there had been a sea of slate, now moonlight spilled a path of rippling silver across the water.

I was so enraptured by the scene, I paid little attention to the growing brightness in the room until my eyes caught a slight movement from the couch. I glanced down, and the sight of the man sculpted by moonlight and shadow took my breath away.

Sergei lay on his back, one arm flung across his forehead, the other hanging over the side of the couch. Shadows masked his eyes and softened the strong line of cheek and jaw, while a white wave of moonlight bathed his bare chest and arms. For a moment, I felt as if I had stumbled upon the statue of a young god, and somehow, through the magic of moonlight or seaspell, cold marble had come to life. I stood motionless, my artist's eyes entranced by the symmetry of his body—the sinuous curve of neck and shoulders, the smoothly-muscled chest and broad lift of his rib cage. The wine-silk pajamas were low about his hips, while the blankets, kicked off during his restless sleep, lay in dusky folds about his feet, like an abandoned artist's drape.

As if to remind me that he was indeed flesh and blood, the man on the couch tensed, tossed his head and mumbled some Russian phrase. I told myself I should go, but I couldn't move. Nor could I draw my eyes away.

Sergei moaned again, and like one in a dream, I moved forward to kneel on the rug beside him. Watching the rapid rise and fall of his chest, I realized my own breathing was keeping pace with his. In my mind, I saw it all again, his outstretched hand reaching toward me across the waves, and I felt his silent cry for help. Now, as I had then, I took his hand in mine.

For a few seconds, Sergei seemed unaware of my touch, then his fingers tightened in a painful grip born of the dream's desperation. I winced, but didn't pull my hand away, wanting only to take his pain and make it mine. A moment later, his fingers relaxed and his eyes opened, appearing black and fathomless in the moonlight.

If he had spoken, asked me what I thought I was doing here in the middle of the night, I would have been forced to make some lame excuse and the spell would have been broken. But he didn't. Instead, lifting my hand, he placed it on his chest where I could feel the warmth of his skin and steady beat of his heart. His other hand found its way to my hair, where his long fingers gently sifted through the strands.

The spell which held us there was fragile as the moonlight. Sometime later, his eyes closed, and the weight of his hand on my neck grew heavy and relaxed.

In a few short hours, morning would come and Sergei would go out of my life. There would be time then for regrets. But now, wrapped in moonlight and the silken silence of the night, it was easy to forget everything but the wonder of his nearness. For however long this moment might last, I was not Cassie Graves . . . only *Kasenya.*

I leaned my head against his side, watching him sleep and breathed the name I had been longing to say. *"Seriozha. . . ."*

It was still dark when I left him and crept back to my room. Shivering from emotion more than the cold, I sat on the edge of the bed and picked up my wristwatch. Three-forty. I had nearly two hours before it would be light enough to go down to the beach, and there was no question of sleeping now. Not when my mind was filled with potent images of the man sleeping downstairs. I had no explanation for what had passed between us or why. I only knew emotions were swelling inside me, aching for expression and release. Smiling in the darkness, I got off the bed and quickly crossed the hall to the dormer room where I'd unpacked my art supplies. I fumbled through the cardboard boxes, grabbed a large sketch pad and some pencils, then hurried back to my room and switched on the lamp. Sitting in bed with pillows at my back and the sketch pad propped against my knees, I took a sharpened pencil and went to work. My bandaged hand and sore fingers were soon forgotten as the portrait began to take shape. I didn't try to analyze how my memory was able to reproduce the image of a man I had known for a few hours; I was conscious only of the creative energy flowing from my mind to my fingers to the paper, and the piercing physical pleasure I felt in sketching Sergei's strong Slavic face.

I paused, erased, then gave a little more slant to the brows; added a touch of shadow to the curve of his jaw. His mouth needed a hint of passion and sadness. My fingers raced on, intent on capturing the masculine beauty of his body. Along with the thrill of creativity, I couldn't deny the sense of guilty pleasure that rushed over me, almost as if I were touching him instead of the paper, but there was no stopping now. . .

Soft gray light filtering into the room warned me it was past time to leave, and I reluctantly set the sketch aside. I got out of bed, stretching tense neck and shoulder muscles, then propped the pad against the pillows and stepped back to examine my work. I was still feeling too heady from an artistic high to be totally objective, but the canny critic inside me knew the portrait was good. Better than anything I'd done in recent months.

I absently unbuttoned my nightshirt and was slipping it off my shoulders when the vision of a larger portrait burst into my mind.

Çolors sharpened . . . images intensified . . . I saw white gulls wheeling against a sunset sky, slivers of gold on their wings . . . and *Seriozha* emerging from the sea, his tanned legs and body gleaming against the white foam and emerald phosphorescence of the waves.

I shivered, suddenly conscious of my own nakedness, and quickly rebuttoned the nightshirt. The portrait could wait, but dawn would not. Thinking now only of the need to hurry, I stepped into my Levis, slipped a heavy cardigan over the nightshirt for warmth and grabbed my shoes.

The morning breeze was brisk and chill as I descended the wooden steps down to the beach. Already the sky was dove-gray, and the clouds over the ocean held a faint tinge of pink. At the bottom of the steps, I clambered over rocks and driftwood, then sprinted toward the slick. The tide was still out, and the wet sand was hard as asphalt under my feet. The song of the gulls seemed to mock my need to hurry. This is reality, they cried—the rough cadence of waves, fresh sea air and a solitary stretch of sand. The threat of discovery, secret police and haunting, dark brown eyes were only products of a dream.

Around the point, the cabin cruiser was starkly visible against the black rocks and brightening sky, a tangible reminder that last night's events were no dream. As yet, the gulls and I had the beach to ourselves, but I knew it wouldn't be long before some beachcomber appeared.

Using the large, humped rock as a reference point, I began my search. Barely five minutes later, I found one of the life jackets wedged among some driftwood and a slimy mass of seaweed. I bent down and tried to pull it free, but one of the ties was tangled in the seaweed and some fishing line. Balancing one foot on a rock and the other on a log, I grabbed hold of the jacket and pulled harder. The log shifted and the tie gave way with a suddenness that sent me sprawling over backwards on the sand. I got up and quickly glanced around, but two gulls were the only witnesses to my lack of dignity. And they were more interested in fighting over a crab leg.

Another ten minutes' searching produced nothing, and it was

light enough now I didn't dare stay longer. Clutching the life jacket close to me and keeping a wary eye on the cliffs, I ran around the point on dry sand and headed for the hillside steps at a dead run.

Minutes later, panting and breathless, I slipped in the back door with my find. As I tiptoed across the kitchen to the utility room, the silent house seemed to assure me that my early morning errand had gone undetected. Once the life jacket was stowed safely out of sight in the broom closet, I took off my sweater and brushed the damp sand off my nightshirt and the seat of my jeans.

The men's clothes were still sitting on top of the washing machine. I had intended to take care of that chore last night, then forgot all about it. Sergei's jeans and sweatshirt were wrinkled and stiff with salt but shouldn't be any worse for wear after a good washing. I seriously doubted whether the professor's jacket and trousers would ever be the same. I stuffed their clothes into the machine, then reached for the box of detergent on a shelf above the washer.

"Where have you been?"

I dropped the box with a gasp, spilling detergent down the front of the washer, the floor and my feet.

"*Skaziti!*" Sergei demanded from the doorway, a suspicious frown narrowing his brows. "Tell me what it is that interests you so early in the day."

"I — I went to the beach to look for the life jackets . . . and my things."

"Life jackets?"

I nodded and opened the closet to show him. "I thought you and Nikolai might be safer if whoever finds the boat doesn't realize there were any survivors. I only found one though. I'm pretty sure everything else was washed away by the tide."

The wariness was gone as he stepped toward me. "I am sorry to startle you. When I heard you leave . . . I had other thoughts."

And I had thought things would be different in the light of morning; that my attraction to him would be something faintly remembered, like waking from a dream and feeling the events and images fade into vague impressions. Seeing him now, tousle-haired and barefoot, with stubble on his jaw and a curious warmth lighting those dark eyes, the feeling was stronger than ever.

I glanced away and brushed some of the spilled soap into the machine, then poured more detergent without bothering to measure it. "I — I meant to wash these last night, but so much was happening —"

"It does not matter," he said gently.

I fumbled with the dials on the washer, then reached past him to get a broom and dustpan out of the closet.

Sergei smiled and took them from me. "Once again, I am making a mess for you. If you will permit — ?"

I surrendered the broom with a breathless, "Spa-se-ba."

His smile deepened, rewarding my attempt to speak his language. For a moment, we just stood there, smiling at each other, then I decided it was time to calm things down into words.

"Is the professor still sleeping?"

"Soundly, yes."

"That's good. I mean — I'm glad he's getting some rest. Are you hungry? I can cook you some breakfast. . . ."

"It is early still. I will wait for Kolya."

"What about coffee? Or tea —" I broke off, realizing I was beginning to sound like a stewardess.

"Tea would be nice, if you will also have some."

I smiled and floated into the kitchen.

As I filled the teakettle, I watched out the corner of one eye while Sergei swept up the detergent and dumped it into a wastebasket. I put the kettle on the stove, then ran self-conscious fingers through my hair. Windblown, without a speck of makeup, I must look a sight. And my clothes! I glanced down at the jade green nightshirt and nearly groaned outloud. In my haste, I'd buttoned the first button in the second buttonhole, leaving a lopsided gap and ample room for embarrassment. I finished rebuttoning the shirt only scant seconds before Sergei entered the room.

He sat down at the table and ran a hand over its worn wooden surface. I followed his glance as he took in the white walls and blue-painted woodwork, the sand dollars on the windowsill, and the dried starfish on top of the fridge. "This is a pleasant room."

"I've always thought so."

"Your grandfather loved the sea."

I smiled and nodded, taking a package of herbal tea from the cupboard. "He was captain of a charter fishing boat for many years."

"The sea is part of this house. I see it in every room. I especially admire your painting which hangs over the fireplace."

I stared at him in surprise. "Thank you. I — it was done a long time ago."

"You have a gift," he said.

They were my grandfather's words, spoken in the same direct way, but from a man I barely knew. Tears suddenly stung my eyelids, and I was glad when the teakettle's insistant whistle gave me an excuse to turn around and brush them away. By the time I'd poured the boiling water and put the tea bags in to steep, my emotions were under control again.

"Cream or sugar?"

"Please."

I brought our cups to the table, and Sergei pulled out the chair next to his.

"I am sorry about the death of your grandfather. I neglected to say so last night."

I sat down and slowly stirred my tea. "We were very close."

"Do you have other family?"

"My parents live in Eugene; that's a city about a hundred miles southeast of here. And I have two married sisters, Charlotte and Emily."

"Like the Bronte's?" he asked, smiling.

I stared in frank amazement. "You know the Bronte's?"

"Of course. In University library there are many books by English and American writers."

"I guess I shouldn't be so surprised, but somehow, I never imagined a Russian sitting down to read *Jane Eyre* or *Wuthering Heights.*"

"English is required language in most Soviet schools," he told me. "I suspect that Soviet students may know more about English literature than many Americans."

I conceded his point with a smile.

Sergei sipped the tea, then asked, "Have you read *Doctor Zhivago?*"

"Twice. It's a wonderful book."

"That is one thing I hoped to buy during my stay here. Pasternak's novel is no longer banned in Soviet Union, but I have not yet been able to find a copy." His broad shoulders lifted in an expressive shrug, then he glanced out the window. "I suppose now that no longer matters. . . ."

Watching his face, I felt sure his thoughts must be thousands of miles away. "What part of the Soviet Union are you from?"

"I have been studying and working seven years at University in Leningrad, but I was born in Riga—a city on the Baltic Sea."

"Does your family still live in Riga?"

He stared down at his cup. "I have a mother and younger brother there."

"I'm sorry. I shouldn't have asked about your family. That must be very painful for you."

"Right now, I am feeling shock more than pain, like the feeling which comes after —" He paused, searching for the word to express himself, then turned to me. "What is English word you call after an arm or leg has been cut off?"

"Amputation," I said, suppressing a shudder.

He nodded. "Amputation. That is how I feel. I know I will never see them again, but the loss is so sudden—it comes so fast, the mind feels no pain—only numbness. Later, the pain will come. For all my life, I will feel pain for that which was cut off."

Without thinking, I reached for his hand. The touch rekindled memories of our time together during the night. I could see it burning in his eyes, yet he said nothing. His fingers moved to tighten around my wrist in wordless understanding, and I knew then he would not lessen what had passed between us with common words. Last night was something to be remembered in thought, a glance or the touch of a hand.

"Tell me about your painting," he said after a moment. "Is it profession or hobby for you?"

"A little of both, I suppose." I picked up my cup and took a steadying sip of tea, amazed that I could still feel the pleasant pressure where his hand had held my wrist. "I got my master's last month, and now I'd like to do some professional illustrating."

"What kind of books would you illustrate?"

I hesitated, then smiled at him. "For a long time, I've had an idea for a book of sea legends and folk tales."

Sergei nodded his approval. "Your grandfather would be proud of such a book."

"I was thinking of dedicating it to him."

"That is as it should be. May I ask, do you have plans for any Russian legends in this book?"

As of right now, I thought. Aloud, I told him, "I'm just starting to gather material. Do you know some?"

He smiled. "I know many. Since the Revolution, most *skomorksy*, that is to say, the storytellers have died out, but their stories live on." His long fingers cradled the cup as he thought for a moment. "I think to a Russian, the river is loved even more than the sea. In his wanderings, the river showed him his way. He built his home along her bank. She was road to the traveller in summer and winter. The river made men brothers."

I smiled and rested an elbow on the table, enjoying the poetry in his words and voice.

"Rivers and lakes had their mysteries as well," he went on. "The early Russians believed that spirit of the river murmured when pleased, and roared when angry. Some contained spirits who were green-bearded, old and ugly. When drunk, these spirits made the river overflow. Othertimes, they would guide fish into fishermen's nets." He paused and his dark eyes were intent on my face. "A favorite legend of mine tells of the *rusalka.*"

"Rusalka? What a lovely name. Who is that?"

Sergei's eyes moved over my face and hair. "*Rusalka* is a water nymph, a beautiful naked girl with silken hair, skin like moonlight and emerald eyes. Legend says her laughter and songs would charm men so that some would gladly drown themselves for her sake."

I felt as if I were the one drowning, lost in the depths of his eyes. When one of his hands cupped my chin, I went willingly toward him, thoughts whirling. *What am I doing? He's going to kiss me . . . This is crazy, but I want him to . . . I want him to . . .*

As I closed my eyes, a shrill ringing jerked us out of the warm depths of pleasure and a secluded forest pool, back to the surface and the simple sunlit kitchen. I jumped up from the table and reached the telephone before the end of the second ring.

"Good morning, darling!"

"Kevin — ?"

His voice was like a cold douse of reality poured over my heated emotions.

"Did I wake you?"

"I — no, I've been up for a while."

"I'm sorry to call so early, but with the meetings I've got scheduled this morning, it was my only chance. Besides, I knew I couldn't begin my day without hearing your voice. . . ."

Guilt washed over me as I listened to him, while at the table, Sergei watched me with interest and concern. The bald fact came to me that ever since last night, I hadn't given my fiance a single moment's thought. Not one.

"Cassie, are you all right?"

"Yes . . . yes, I'm all right."

"You sound different. Out of breath or something."

"I've been down to the beach for a walk, that's all."

I could hear the smile in his voice. "I should have known that's where you'd be. What are your plans for today?"

"Plans?" My voice rose, and I fought to keep it light. "Well, I'll probably spend most of the morning painting. Why?"

"I just wanted to be able to picture you in my mind while I'm sitting in those boring meetings. Cass?"

"Yes."

"I've been thinking. What would you say if I left a plane ticket at the airport for you? We could have dinner together, spend the evening —"

"I'm sorry, Kevin, but I — I can't. I'm going to be awfully busy today."

"I thought you said you were only going to be painting."

"I am! That's just it. I have the most wonderful idea for a new portrait. I did a preliminary sketch this morning and . . . well, you know how it is when I get started on something —" I caught Sergei's glance and said with more desperation than I intended, "I can't leave. That's all."

"Cass, are you sure you're all right?"

"I'm fine."

"Something's wrong."

"Nothing's wrong! Look, I'm sorry to disappoint you, but I can't pack up and go flying off to New York when I barely got here."

"I know, I know. It's just — I go crazy thinking about you when we're not together. I can't help it if I love you too much."

I stood very still, feeling more miserable by the second. "Kevin, please. . . ."

"Sorry." I heard him draw a quick breath and add with forced cheerfulness, "Well, I'd better get going. Have a good time painting today."

"I will, and — and I hope your meetings aren't too boring."

"Just boring enough, right?" His bright tone was edged with sarcasm. "Will I be disturbing your work if I call you tonight?"

I bit down on my lower lip. "Of course not. Good-bye, Kevin." I hung up quickly and stood there, my hand still on the receiver, my face to the wall.

I heard Sergei get up from the table and walk toward me.

"That was my fiance," I said, not giving him a chance to speak. My smile felt stiff and forced as I turned to face him. "He's on a business trip in New York, so you and Nikolai don't need to worry about anything."

"*Kasenya*, I am sorry if —"

"No — I'm sorry. I don't know what's the matter with me this morning. I keep forgetting things. . . ." Like Kevin and the fact that I'm engaged, I thought miserably. "You'd probably like to wash up or something."

"I would, yes."

"The bathroom's down the hall next to my grandfather's room — or, if you'd like a shower, there's one in the upstairs bathroom."

"*Spaseba*. A shower would be fine."

I turned away. "I'll get you some towels —"

Chapter 5

I WALKED OVER to the table and stared dismally at Sergei's cup and saucer. What must he think of me—to permit, even encourage such intimacy, when I was engaged to marry someone else? If I'd been wearing my ring, things might have been different, but I'd taken it off last night, the way I always did before painting.

I sat down and ran a fingertip around the rim of Sergei's cup. A tangible reminder of Kevin's presence in my life might have changed what just happened, but would a ring make any difference in the way I felt? How could I love one man and want another to kiss me? I should be grateful Kevin's phone call had prevented that kiss from ever happening. But I wasn't. With a quiet moan, I closed my eyes and put my head in my hands.

"Excuse me —?"

My head jerked up and I swung around to see Dr. Petrovsky standing in the kitchen doorway.

"Excuse me," he said again, venturing a few steps into the room. "But I was wondering if something is wrong?"

"No . . . no, I'm fine."

He considered this with a slight frown. "A moment ago, I pass Sergei in the hall. He also insists he is fine, yet his face wears the same troubled expression." Dr. Petrovsky made his way to the table and sat down in the chair Sergei had vacated. "Is there something you are keeping from me—bad news perhaps?"

I smiled to reassure him. "There isn't any bad news. Honestly, I would have told you."

"I worry too much, I know," he admitted. "But a few minutes ago, when the telephone rang. . . ."

"That was my fiance."

The professor straightened slightly, his hazel eyes intent on my face.

"Everything's fine," I said. "Kevin's in New York on business, so there's nothing to worry about."

Nikolai acknowledged this with a nod. "Forgive me, but I am also wondering if you and Sergei reached Paul Miklos?"

Embarrassed color replaced my blank expression. "Well . . . we sort of . . . forgot."

A heavy spasm of coughing interrupted the professor's reply, and I hurried to get him a glass of water. He drank it gratefully, trying to catch his breath.

"Are you all right?"

He nodded and cleared his throat. "It is nothing—only a summer cold."

"Are you sure? After last night. . . ."

Nikolai smiled and patted my hand. "There is no cause for concern. But please, if I might trouble you to telephone Paul Miklos?"

"I'll call him right now. What do you want me to say?"

"For the moment, do not mention where we are. Just tell him Sergei and I are seeking political asylum and would like your government's protection. If he agrees, I will speak to him."

I nodded and went to the phone. After the eighth ring, I hung up and faced the professor. "I guess our next move is to call the Custom's Office. Someone there is bound to know where Miklos can be reached."

"Can we do that now?"

I glanced at the kitchen clock. "I don't think anyone will be in this early. Not until nine or ten, anyway."

"Then we will wait," he said with a sigh. "After so many years, another hour should not be too difficult."

In spite of his words, frustration and disappointment were evident on his face.

"Is there anything I can do to make you more comfortable?

Perhaps you'd like a hot bath while I cook breakfast."

"Such kindness. You are spoiling me, Cassandra." Weariness marked his movements as he rose from the chair, but his smile was warm. "Your grandfather was a most fortunate man."

Sunlight streamed through the kitchen windows, mellow rays mingling with moist steam rising from cups of hot coffee and a platter of scrambled eggs and sausage.

Nikolai Petrovsky raised his glass of orange juice, smiling at Sergei and me. "I should like to propose toast. *Ja mir i druzhbu.* To peace and friendship."

"To peace and friendship."

Sergei's deep voice echoed the words along with mine, our hands brushed lightly and our glasses clinked in the golden haze.

At that moment, the length of such an unlikely friendship mattered little. The mere fact that our lives had touched at all seemed a small miracle. Throughout the meal, I found myself avoiding the clock, as if that could somehow push time away or slow its passage. Inside, I felt the urgency of making that telephone call to the Customs Office, yet I was selfish enough to wish our meal and simple conversation could last a little longer.

"Excellent sausage," Nikolai told me for the third time.

I smiled and offered him the last two on the platter as Sergei reached for a piece of toast. Our eyes met briefly before he glanced down to butter the bread, but there was nothing more than passive politeness in his expression. Why I should find that disappointing I refused to consider. Instead, I shoved back my chair with a grating scrape and said, "I forgot to put the jam on the table. I'll get you some."

Not bothering to spoon the preserves into a separate dish, I took the whole bottle and set it in front of him. That same moment, the back door burst open and Mrs. Davis bustled into the room.

"Cassie dear, you'll never guess what's happened! There's a boat in the —" The woman stopped short to stare at Sergei and the professor. "Oh . . . excuse me. I wouldn't have bothered you if I'd known you had company."

For a heart-stopping moment we all stared at one another—the two Russians in shocked silence and Mrs. Davis in round-eyed curiosity as she took in the men sitting at my breakfast table, dressed in robe and pajamas. Before she could start asking questions, I whipped on a smile and said the first thing that popped into my head.

"You're not bothering me, and—and this really isn't company. Mrs. Davis, I'd like you to meet my fiance, Kevin, and his father, Grant Barlow."

Mrs. Davis' eyes widened even more. "Oh, my! Cassie, you never told me your young man was so . . . so . . ." She shook her head, then fluttered a smile in Sergei's direction. "You're not at all what I expected."

Sergei smiled and rose to shake her hand, but wisely said nothing. When the woman turned to the professor, Nikolai bent over her plump fingers and bestowed a gallant kiss.

"Oh, my!" she said again, blushing a girlish pink. "This really is a surprise. But I thought you said your fiance was away on a business trip."

"He is—I mean, he was—that is, he —"

"The trip—it was cut short," Sergei filled in, slipping an arm around my waist. "So I decide to make a surprise for Cassandra."

Mrs. Davis beamed at him, so delighted by this she didn't seem to notice his marked accent. "Well, I can see just to look at you two that it was a pleasant surprise. Strange, I didn't hear your car though. What time did you get here?"

I felt a stab of panic and my mind went blank.

Before Mrs. Davis could say another word, Sergei sat down and pulled me onto his lap. "When I am with Cassandra, I forget the time," he murmured against my neck.

"Now, Cassie, there's no need to look so embarrassed," Mrs. Davis said with a chuckle. "It isn't as if I haven't seen two people in love before." Turning to the professor, she added, "I hope you know what a wonderful daughter-in-law you're getting."

Nikolai smiled and nodded, "I do indeed."

"Don't let me keep you folks from your breakfast," she went on, settling herself at the end of the table. "I've already had mine, so you go right ahead. You might pass me that last little slice of toast though. And that strawberry jam looks real tasty."

I handed her the toast, then the jam, thinking I could use that as an excuse to slip off Sergei's lap, but his arms around my waist were solidly secure.

"You know, I always thought Cassie here was a mite too picky when it came to young men," Mrs. Davis told the professor. "Had her head in the clouds most the time." She slapped a spoonful of jam on the toast, then gave Nikolai a sly nudge with her elbow. "I never did believe in any 'Prince Charmings' myself, but I'll be the first to admit your son is worth the wait. They make a wonderful couple."

I sat in rigid silence, certain my face must be ten shades past scarlet, while Dr. Petrovsky responded with a warm smile and calmly sipped his coffee, from all outward appearances, completely at ease with the situation.

"How long will you be staying?" Mrs. Davis went on. "George and I'd be tickled to have you come over for dinner some time."

Nikolai spoke into his coffee cup. "Thank you, but our plans are uncertain just now."

I drew a tense breath, wondering how long we could keep up this charade before she noticed their accents or asked something we couldn't answer.

"Try to relax, *Kasenya,*" Sergei whispered in my ear. "You are stiff like poker. Put your arm around my neck."

Keeping my gaze fixed straight ahead, I did as he asked. When I leaned against him, my fears melted into pleasure. There was warmth where the curve of my body met his. Warmth and a sense of wonder that it should feel so right. My fingers brushed against the softness of his hair, and his quickened breathing filled me with a heady rush of emotion.

"Well, I guess I'd better be on my way and let you two lovebirds have some time together. Something tells me you'd better keep an eye on these two," she told the professor with a wink.

Nikolai rose politely as Mrs. Davis offered him her hand.

"Now don't forget about that dinner invitation. Our house is the first one down the road on your right, with the blue shutters and— my lands!" Muriel Davis clapped a hand to her mouth and stared at me. "I nearly forgot why I came over in the first place! There's a boat trapped in the rocks just around the point! George spotted it a while back, and I called the Coast Guard. They're on their way now to check things out."

Sergei's arms fell away from me, and I got to my feet. "Do you know if anyone is hurt?" I asked, hoping my voice sounded no more than naturally curious.

"There isn't a soul on board, and so far as I know, there haven't been any bodies wash up on the beach. Kinda gives you a creepy feeling, doesn't it? The Coast Guard'll probably send a helicopter down from Astoria. It's easier to spot bodies from the air, you know. Well, I'd better be off. I just thought you ought to know in case someone wants to use your place for access to the beach."

Sergei rose politely as I walked her to the door, his face a tight mask of control.

"It's been a pleasure meeting you both," Mrs. Davis said, bestowing a dazzling smile on the two Russians. Halfway out, she whispered in a low tone, "Take my advice, honey, and move your wedding date up a month."

Her parting remark was lost in the taut silence behind me.

"Mrs. Davis is a simple woman, but she is not stupid," Nikolai commented with a frown. "Soon she will realize we have no car and other questions will follow."

"How long before the Coast Guard will come?" Sergei asked me.

"I'm not sure. It depends on how long ago she called." I drew a tense breath and tried to think. "We might have ten minutes . . . maybe less."

Sergei turned to Nikolai with a grim nod. "We should leave now."

"No!" I reached for his arm in a panic. "Leaving now won't solve anything."

"It will protect you," he said quietly.

"Sergei is right. If we stay, it will only make more trouble."

I let go Sergei's arm and fought to keep my voice calm. "If you leave now, how will you get in touch with Paul Miklos? And where will you go? There's nothing but forests and cliffs for miles. Oceanside is the nearest town, and it's only a resort community."

Nikolai hesitated, worry deepening in his face.

"There doesn't have to be any trouble as long as you stay out of sight," I assured him. "My grandfather's room is probably the safest place. The windows all face the cliff so no one will see you."

"But the Coast Guard —" Sergei insisted.

"The Coast Guard will be looking for bodies in the water or survivors along the beach. They won't be searching houses."

"All of this does not change the fact that Mrs. Davis has seen us," he said.

"Mrs. Davis thinks she's seen my fiance and his father. By the time she finds out any different, you'll be gone."

Nikolai shook his head as he looked at me. "Dear Cassandra, I truly wish everything could be simple as you say, but there are other factors —" He covered his mouth to cough, and the spell left him gasping.

"One of the factors we need to consider is your health," I said when Nikolai regained his breath. "As far as I'm concerned, the only place you should go is straight to bed."

Sergei put a supporting arm around his friend's shoulder. *"Kasenya* is right. When you are feeling stronger, we will make our plans."

Nikolai nodded heavily and allowed himself to be led from the room.

Once the men were safely out of sight, I hurried back to the kitchen to load the breakfast dishes in the dishwasher. I glanced about the room, double-checking for any tell-tale evidence that I was not alone. Their clothes were still in the dryer. No problem there. Their shoes! I dashed back to the living room and nearly collided with Sergei who was picking up both pair from the hearth.

He straightened up and gave me a close look. "It is difficult, I know, but you must try not to worry so. It will show in your eyes."

I sank down on the couch with a shaky sigh. "But what if I

make a mistake—say or do the wrong thing?"

"Mistakes are less likely if you speak the truth as much as possible. Is much better that way."

"Even if the truth puts you and Nikolai in danger?"

Sergei set the shoes on the floor and sat down beside me. "If you cannot speak freely, withholding part of the truth is still better than a lie. Say what people expect you to say. Do what you see others do, and keep your thoughts to yourself."

I considered his words. "Is that what you do?"

"Sometimes. It keeps one out of trouble. This morning, for example, it is good idea for you to behave as if we were not here. Did you not tell your fiance that you would be painting?"

"Yes."

"Then that is what you must do. And when Coast Guard arrives, would it not be natural curiosity to interest yourself in their activities?"

"I guess so, but what if I run into Mrs. Davis? She'll want to know why you're not with me."

"Mrs. Davis is a problem, I agree." He leaned back against the cushions and thought a moment. "It is best you avoid her, but if this is not possible, you might say my father is tired from our journey, and I will join you later. Again, this is mostly truth."

"You make it sound so simple, but—I've never done anything like this before."

A teasing light came into his dark eyes. "For one with no experience, you have performed well."

Warmth rushed into my cheeks as I caught his meaning. "Oh . . . that."

"This morning, when Mrs. Davis came, it could have been all over for us," he said seriously. "You were very quick . . . very good."

From overhead, the rhythmic whirring of metal blades penetrated the room's quiet and brought me quickly to my feet.

"They're here! I'd better get my paints."

Sergei laughed and rose also. "Unless it is helicopter you wish to paint instead of the ocean, there is no rush, *Kasenya.*"

I laughed at my own foolishness, and he nodded his approval.

"Much better. To see a smile in your eyes instead of fear." Sergei reached out to touch my face, caught himself, and bent down to retrieve the shoes instead. "I will go now," he said stiffly.

I stood for a long moment after he had gone, feeling strangely bereft. For the second time in a short space of hours, Sinbad had set my emotions adrift on a strange new sea, leaving me longing for a touch that never happened.

Chapter 6

NOT FIFTEEN MINUTES after Sergei had left me, a loud knock sounded on the front door. Thankfully, I was dressed by that time and gathering up my paints and brushes. Before the knock came, I was also congratulating myself on feeling so calm. The sharp rapping immediately changed all that.

Still clutching a tube of cadmium yellow, I hurried downstairs, unlocked the front door and opened it a few inches.

Two crewmen from the Coast Guard stood outside. Crewman Kelly, according to the name badge on his jacket, was tall and lanky with a ruddy complexion and sandy brown hair. Jaworski, the man on the steps behind him, had smooth, dark hair and a thick mustache that lent him a piratic look.

"Morning." The sandy-haired crewman gave me a polite smile. "Are you Cassie Graves?"

"Yes."

"One of your neighbors, a Mrs. Davis, reported a boat was trapped in some rocks near here. She said your property has some stairs down to the beach. Do you mind if we use them?"

"Not at all." I stepped onto the porch and pointed to the grove of fir trees below the house. "There's a path just beyond those trees."

"Thanks." Crewman Kelly glanced toward the sweep of ocean beyond Winwood Cottage. "Your place has a pretty good view of the beach. Did you notice anything last night or this morning?"

My hesitation was slight. "I just got here yesterday, and it was so stormy I didn't go out much. Mrs. Davis mentioned the boat when she came by earlier. I'm sorry I can't be more help."

The dark-haired crewman's frank, appraising look held more male interest than anything else. I turned a smiling glance his way. "Feel free to come and go as you want. I was going down to the beach myself in a few minutes to paint."

Kelly gave me a friendly nod, then headed down the porch steps and across the lawn.

"We'll probably see you down there," Jaworski called over his shoulder, giving me a hopeful smile.

I nodded, shut the door, and headed straight for my grand-father's room. Sergei answered my quiet knock.

"Everything's all right," I told him. "That was the Coast Guard, but they only wanted to use the steps down to the beach."

"And why is this all right?" he demanded. "Why do they come here, to this place, instead of another?"

Behind him, Dr. Petrovsky was sitting up in bed, a book lying open in his lap and a pale mask of worry on his face.

"There's no public access to the beach below us," I explained, "except for a steep trail down the cliff—and that's on the opposite end from the boat. Mrs. Davis told them about the steps."

Sergei's frown lifted, but his voice was still wary. "And did they question you?"

"A little. One of the crewmen asked if I'd noticed anything—meaning the boat, of course. I told him I hadn't gone out much since yesterday because of the storm."

Sergei nodded, his dark eyes warm with approval.

"Well, I . . . I guess I'd better get my paints and head for the beach. I'll try to find out what I can." I glanced away with some difficulty and turned to the professor. "Is there anything you need before I go? Would you like me to change your bandages?"

"I am most comfortable, and the wound seems to be healing well."

Gulliver chose that moment to leap onto the bed and start kneading a soft nest in the professor's lap with his front paws.

Nikolai smiled and stroked the tom's chin. "Ah, my friend, so you have come back to pay me another visit."

"If Gulliver gets to be too much of a pest, I can put him outside."

"Gulliver. So that is your name. I must say, you look like a cat who has seen many places. Many places indeed."

Gulliver arched his back with pleasure, then settled himself with great dignity on top of the professor's book.

"It seems Gulliver has decided my eyes need a rest from reading," Nikolai told me with a chuckle.

I smiled and turned to Sergei. "I'd better go. I'll be back as soon as I can."

For a moment, he looked as though he wanted to say something, then he shook his head.

"Don't worry," I said, hoping to ease the anxiety in his eyes. "I remember what you told me. Say what people expect me to say. Do what I see others do, and keep my thoughts to myself."

His smile, a little embarrassed as well as pleased, lingered in my mind long after I had left the house.

I set up my easel in a strategic location around the point, with a dramatic view of Cape Meares' rocky headland and the trapped cabin cruiser. The sea was a deep cobalt blue, with a brisk chop on the waves. Above me, cormorants and gulls soared in a moody sky where sunlight and shadow played tag with clouds that couldn't seem to decide whether to huddle together for another rainy conversation or disperse and blow away. Artistically and otherwise, it was perfect. I was able to go through the motions of painting and still observe the Coast Guard's efforts, although my nerves had a hard time of it as the two crewmen searched the same area where I had found the life jacket only a few hours before. The helicopter passed over twice before flying south, and there was a motor life launch cruising the waters as well.

Mrs. Davis must have decided to view the search operation from the convenience of her backyard, because she was nowhere in sight. Except for the crewmen and two elderly agate hunters, there was no one else on the beach.

The two women were well into their sixties, dressed in slacks, scarves and sweatshirts to ward off the chill morning breeze. One was tall and gaunt, traipsing over the gravel beds like a long-legged crane. The other woman skittered about, poking here and darting there like a nervous sanderling.

The sanderling stopped long enough to give my easel a curious glance and ask, "Do you know anything about that boat in the rocks?"

I smiled and tried to come up with an honest answer. "The Coast Guard haven't said much to me. I've only been here a little while."

The crane woman lifted her long neck to give the cabin cruiser an uninterested glance. "It probably belongs to someone over in Garibaldi," she pronounced. "Come on, Sarah, the tide's turned."

The women wandered off in search of more rocky treasures, and I looked seaward at the white froth of a spent wave as it curled onto the sand. She was right about the tide. It wouldn't be long before the sea brought a forced end to the Coast Guard's search of the beach.

Minutes later, the dark-haired crewman wandered over in my direction. After making a superficial inspection of the driftwood logs behind me, he paused to look at my canvas.

"You're really capturing a great mood with that," he said, giving me a winning smile. "Do you come here often to paint?"

"As often as I can."

"Funny, I haven't seen you here before. I usually get over at least once a week to do some perch fishing. I'm Russ Jaworski," he said with another smile. "And you're . . . Cassie, wasn't it?"

I nodded, thinking it would be wise to steer the subject away from me. "How are thing's going? Have you found out anything?"

"Not much, and I doubt we will." He shoved both hands in his pockets and frowned at the trapped cabin cruiser.

"Do you know who owns the boat? The ladies over there thought it might be someone from Garibaldi."

"It's not anybody from around here. She belongs to some professor at OSU."

I hoped my expression was duly surprised. "Really?"

"Yeah, and he didn't even know the boat was gone until we called him a few minutes ago."

I stared at him. "You mean it was stolen?"

"Sure looks that way. How else would a cabin cruiser docked in Yaquina Bay end up on the rocks over a hundred miles north?"

"That is strange. I wonder what happened."

The crewman pointed toward Cape Meares' rugged cliffs. "My guess is she lost power further north, then drifted down with the current. The tide had to be coming in or they never would've made it this close to shore. Had to be sometime last night." His dark eyes scanned the beach where Sergei and I had dragged the professor onto the sand, and I felt myself tense up. "A good swimmer could've made it. Depends how long he was in the water though—" He broke off at the approach of the sandy-haired crewman. "What's up, Kelly?"

"Not much." Kelly gave me an acknowledging glance and said tersely, "Unless you plan on spending the rest of the day out here, you'd better be heading back. Tide's turned."

I shrugged and smiled. "The light's changed anyway. I'll have to come back tomorrow." I began packing up my paints, seemingly unaware of the crewmen's conversation as they sized up the situation.

"What did Harrison say about the boat?" Jaworski asked. "Does he want us to try and pull it off the rocks?"

"Not yet. Depends how tight she's wedged in those rocks. We might tear a hole in her." Kelly turned to me. "Excuse me . . . Miss Graves, wasn't it? Could I ask another favor?"

"Certainly, if I can help. . . ."

"The owner's on his way to check things out. I had the dispatcher give him directions to your place."

"He's coming here?" My voice rose to a shrill, taut pitch.

A puzzled look came into the crewman's eyes. "I hope that's not a problem."

I glanced down and fumbled with the tubes of oil paint, feeling my control crumble into fear. "No . . . no problem. . . ."

"His name's Bill Harrison, and he probably won't get here for a couple of hours," Kelly told me. "Sometime around noon."

"That's fine. . . ." I made a clumsy effort to pick up my easel, and Russ Jaworski stepped forward.

"Here, let me help you with that," he offered, taking the easel from me. "I don't know how you packed it down all those steps without breaking your neck."

I thanked him with a nervous smile, and we started across the sand toward the point. The crewmen's leisurely pace only increased my agitation. Inside, I felt the urgency of getting Sergei and the professor away from Winwood Cottage before Dr. Harrison arrived, while on the outside I was forced to smile and make polite conversation. Jaworski hinted broadly that he'd like to see me again and asked for my telephone number, with the pretense he might need it for Dr. Harrison. Thankfully, we'd reached the house by that time, and the best I could do was pretend I hadn't heard his request.

"Thanks for your help," I said, taking the easel.

"I'll be glad to carry your things inside. . . ."

"No . . . no, I can manage. Thanks anyway."

Kelly must have attributed my nervousness as a response to his friend's none too subtle approach, because he gave Jaworski a pointed look and firmly insisted they wouldn't intrude on my day any further.

Undaunted, Russ Jaworski waved and called a promising, "See you around!" over his shoulder as they headed up the drive toward a Ford Bronco.

Another time, I might have felt complimented by the man's persistance. This morning, I hurried into the house without a backward glance, dumped my easel in the corner of the kitchen and checked the clock. Ten twenty-eight. If we could reach Paul Miklos within the next hour, I could drive Sergei and Nikolai to Astoria myself. The sooner they received the government's protection, the better.

I went to the wall phone, then paused, receiver in hand. Before calling Astoria, I really ought to tell the men about Harrison's arrival. And if we were going to leave soon, they would need their clothes. I hung up the phone, trying to sort through my jumbled thoughts. Clothes first, then the news about Dr. Harrison, and then the phone call.

With their clothes in my arms, I headed for my grandfather's room. The door opened before I could lift a hand to knock, and

Sergei stepped into the hall. "Kolya is sleeping," he whispered, shutting the door behind him.

"Is he all right?"

"He seems to be, but he is very weary. Did you learn anything from the Coast Guard's investigation?" he asked, as we moved away from the room.

"Right now, they're assuming the boat was stolen, and they don't expect to find any survivors."

"If they know the boat was stolen, they must also know its owner."

I nodded. "Dr. Harrison is on his way here to check things out."

Sergei's shocked reaction mirrored my own a few minutes earlier. "Here? Why should Harrison come here?"

"The Coast Guard gave him my name and address. I'm sorry, but when they asked me, I couldn't think of a good reason to refuse." I leaned against the wall with a sigh, holding their clothes against me. "At least Dr. Harrison won't be arriving for a couple of hours. We still have time to reach Paul Miklos, and if things can be worked out, I'll drive you and Nikolai up to Astoria this morning. We could be gone before Harrison gets here."

Sergei stepped closer. "You would do this?"

"Of course. . . ."

He gave a disbelieving shake of his head.

"What's wrong? Do you think Nikolai would object?"

Sergei leaned one hand on the wall beside me, and I felt the full force of his dark-eyed gaze. "Why?" he asked in a low tone.

"Why?"

"You answer as if I were making a simple request of no consequence. But this is not simple. And what happens may be of very serious consequence."

"I know. . . ."

"And still you say, of course?"

I nodded slowly.

"Then still I must ask why."

My lips parted, but I had no answer for him. I'd never really stopped to think why I was doing any of this. Something inside . . . an emotion stronger than myself, but how could I find words for a feeling?

The longer I looked into his eyes, the less important an answer seemed to be, and when his dark head leaned closer, I totally forgot the question.

A rhythmic thudding suddenly invaded the silence, and we both glanced up with a start. The sound grew louder as it passed overhead, then diminished to a faint drone in the distance.

"The helicopter must be heading back to Astoria," I said, wishing my voice weren't so breathless and unsteady.

Sergei reached for the clothes in my arms, his hands lingering on mine for a warm moment. "Would you place the call to Customs while I dress? Perhaps we can give Kolya some good news when he awakens."

It took five times before I dialed the number correctly, and even then, I didn't have the faintest idea what to say. The rapid drumming of my heart seemed much louder than the bored male voice who answered, "Customs and Immigration."

"Good morning. I . . . I'd like to speak with Paul Miklos, please."

A loud click answered my request, followed by a mindless rendition of a Beatles' tune. Half a minute later, a woman's voice mercifully ended the Beatles' massacre.

"Paul Miklos' office. May I help you?"

"This is Cassie Graves calling. May I speak with Paul, please?"

"I'm sorry. Mr. Miklos isn't in the office today."

"Oh . . . well, do you have a number where he can be reached? It's very important."

"I'm sorry. Mr. Miklos is out of town and won't be back in the office until Monday. If you'd like to leave a message, I'll be glad to have him call you —"

"No, thanks. I'll — I'll call back Monday."

I hung up the phone and sagged against the counter. Now what? Today was only Thursday. Having Sergei and the professor stay here for nearly four more days was out of the question. But where could they go?

"Miklos refuses to help?"

I straightened up to see Sergei standing in the kitchen doorway, dressed in the jeans and sweatshirt, his body tense as a drawn bow. His expression was equally rigid.

"He's not there," I said. "He's out of town until Monday."

Sergei crossed to the window, and there was something of a caged animal in his restless pacing. "We cannot stay. The risk. . . ."

"I know. There must be something else we can do —"

"You have done enough," he said flatly. "I cannot allow you to carry our burdens any longer."

I stared at him, feeling the cold stirrings of fear inside. "What are you going to do?"

"What we do is no longer your concern. I think perhaps it is better if you do not know our plans."

"But it is my concern! I mean . . . I know Paul Miklos being gone complicates things, but the situation's not hopeless. What about Dr. Harrison? Have you thought of asking him for help? There might be something he —"

Sergei waved away my suggestion with a firm sweep of his hand. "Harrison's help is not a thing to consider. To do so would involve the University, and that presents other difficulties . . . complications. If Harrison were to assist in our defection, the repercussions could be very serious. It would harm his reputation, perhaps even cost him his job. And it would mean a certain end to further scientific exchanges. Do you understand?"

"Yes, but couldn't he help unofficially? Maybe even anonymously?"

"Kolya would never jeopardize their friendship in such a way. And it is possible Dr. Harrison may feel more obligation to the University than to us. For this, we must have respect."

"How can you know that until you ask him? If he's any kind of a decent man, I think there's a good chance he'll place a higher value on friendship than—than loyalty to some institution!"

"Perhaps, but I doubt Kolya will want to risk this."

I crossed over to Sergei and blurted out, "Maybe he won't, but I do! What if I talked to Dr. Harrison? I might be able to learn something . . . you know, feel him out—"

"*Nyet!*" Sergei gripped my arm, his dark eyes blazing. "Your touching of Dr. Harrison will not be required, *Kasenya!*"

I stared at him, startled by his sudden anger. Then it hit me what he was thinking and heat flooded my face.

"You don't understand. I wasn't really going to feel . . . I mean, it's just an expression . . . an idiom —" My frustration and embarrassment dissolved into helpless laughter.

Sergei released my arm, and I sank down onto a chair.

"I'm sorry. I'm not really laughing at you, but the idea of me manhandling some poor professor. . . ." I drew a long breath and smiled at him, feeling better after the release of tension.

Even Sergei's stiff expression had shifted to a crooked grin. "I apologize if my English is not so good."

"Your English is wonderful. It's the language that's crazy. What I was trying to say is, I thought I could learn something from Dr. Harrison. He must be worried sick about you and Nikolai. . . ."

Sergei pulled out a chair and sat down beside me. "Please do not think me ungrateful, *Kasenya*. I know you wish only to help. But I also know Kolya wishes to spare his friend any further involvement."

"Isn't it a little late for that? Whether you like it or not, Bill Harrison is already involved and has been ever since you took his boat." Sergei's tight-lipped silence conceded my point. "Look, I don't know whether he'll be willing to help, but you don't have many other options. Won't you at least think about it?"

"I will consider it," he said reluctantly, "but it is Kolya who must decide."

"Fair enough."

Sergei's dark eyes held mine for an unsettling moment before I glanced down and brushed an imaginary speck from the table's worn surface.

"Do you have other paintings here?"

The question took me by surprise. "Paintings?"

"If it would not present any inconvenience to you, I would enjoy seeing more of your work."

"It's no inconvenience," I said, feeling a pleasant rush of warmth at his request. "I have a few sketches and watercolors upstairs."

The first thing to catch my eye when we reached the top of the stairs was the sketch pad still propped on my bed, with Sergei's portrait in full view. I dived in front of the doorway and motioned to the dormer room across the hall, praying he hadn't noticed. If he had, his face revealed nothing. I quickly shut my bedroom door before following him across the hall.

"My grandfather used this room mostly for storage," I said, keeping my tone light and impersonal, "but I'd like to turn it into an artist's studio."

Sergei glanced about with interest, while I searched through the contents of a cardboard box for my portfolio.

"Will you live here after you are married?" he asked, turning to face me.

"I . . . I don't know. We haven't really talked about it. Kevin works for a computer firm outside Portland, so he might not want to drive that far." I lifted out my portfolio and knelt down on a braided rug. "Actually, Kevin hasn't seen Winwood Cottage yet, but I hope he —"

"Winwood Cottage?" Sergei broke in, sitting down beside me. "Is that what you call this place?"

I nodded, spreading some sketches on the rug in front of us. "My grandfather's name was Winwood. He bought this place for my grandmother. She used to talk a lot about her parents' home over in Scotland, and Grandpa always promised her that someday they'd have their own cottage by the sea."

Sergei picked up one of the pencil sketches. "Is this he?"

I nodded.

"He has the face of a man who keeps his promises." Sergei's dark gaze lifted from the sketch to my face. "In a physical sense, you do not resemble him."

"No. I take after my grandmother Margaret."

His brown eyes warmed and deepened as he looked at me. "She must have been very beautiful."

I glanced down at the portfolio in my hands, feeling oddly breathless and at a loss for words. "I don't remember her very well. After she died, I spent the entire summer here. . . ."

"That must have given your grandfather great comfort," he

said, setting the sketch aside. "What age were you then?"

"About ten. I'll never forget that summer. I cried every night for a week when I had to go back home. It's still that way. No matter how long I'm away or where I'm living, it's like part of me belongs here—or only comes alives when I'm at the cottage. . . ." I broke off, not understanding why I was telling him these things . . . things I had never shared with Kevin.

"There are places which hold the same feeling for me," Sergei said quietly. "Where the welcome I feel is from the house itself, as well as the people."

Neither of us spoke while I removed half a dozen watercolors from the portfolio and arranged them on the braided rug.

"About two months ago, my grandfather wrote and invited me to spend a few weeks in July with him. I was back East at the time, finishing school. He died a week before I got home."

"And so now you keep your promise to him."

"Yes."

Our eyes met in silent understanding, then he turned his attention to the watercolors, examining each one intently. "This one," he said, picking up a seascape I had done of Cape Meares beach. I had used a limited pallette, mostly blues, browns and grays to paint a cloudy sky and choppy sea viewed through the gnarled branches of dead tree. "This is my favorite."

I smiled at him, feeling a secret thrill he had chosen one of my own favorites. "It's yours."

Sergei's eyes sought mine in surprise. "I cannot accept —" he began in a husky tone, then glanced down at the watercolor.

Humiliation burned in my cheeks. When would I learn not to be so impulsive? Not to blurt out whatever came into my head without giving it a moment's thought. I picked up the sketches and carelessly stuffed them back into the portfolio. "I'm sorry. I didn't mean to offend you."

"Such a gift could never give offense, but I must consider my situation. As yet, I do not know what will happen or where I will live. . ." He drew a tight breath and added soberly, ". . . or even if I will have a wall on which to hang your gift."

My throat constricted as I thought of the uncertainty facing him. "Then I'll keep it for you—temporarily. But it's still yours."

The warmth of his hand suddenly covered mine and the bleakness left his eyes. *"Spaseba, Kasenya. . . ."*

"You're welcome . . . *Seriozha.*"

He abruptly released my hand and got to his feet, while I returned the remaining watercolors to the portfolio, trying to preserve the illusion of indifference between us.

"Tell me more of your plans for this room," he said after a moment.

I stood up and set the portfolio on a table. "Before I can do much of anything, I have to finish cleaning out the rest of the boxes . . . and some of the furniture will have to be moved."

"May I help?"

My first impulse was to refuse, but something in his tone stopped the words before they were uttered. The morning's uncertainty and waiting had been hard on me. For Sergei, it must be ten times worse. Why not do something to get our minds off it for a while?

I pointed to a large oval mirror with a tarnished frame. "I was going to put that mirror in the attic, but it's too heavy for me."

Sergei lifted the mirror as easily as if it were made of cardboard, and we went to work. Inside half an hour, most of the boxes were stored or stacked and the extra furniture moved to the attic. Hidden away under a mountain of tied magazines, we found a box of memorabilia from my grandfather's fishing boat. A flood of memories came rushing back as I looked through its contents— wooden floats strung on tough rope, brightly-colored lures, a well-mended net.

I lifted out a tarnished brass bell to show Sergei and found its tone was still hauntingly clear and mellow, like the call of the sea.

"This bell used to be on my grandfather's boat. It seems a shame to store it away."

"A little polishing and it would make a handsome piece."

I handed him the bell and got to my feet. "I think there's some polish in the kitchen."

When I returned, polish and cloth in hand, I found Sergei sitting cross-legged on the floor with the fishing net across his lap, carefully tying some frayed ends. He glanced up at me, echoing what I had said earlier about the bell. "Such a fine net. It seems a shame to store it away."

I thought a moment, then glanced at the wall behind him. "We could drape it across that wall, along with the floats. It would give the room a nautical air, don't you think?"

"Very nautical," he agreed, smiling.

We hung the net together, then Sergei sat down to polish the bell while I set up my easels in the newly-cleared space by the window.

"What was the name of your grandfather's boat?" he asked, rubbing the bell's tarnished surface with strong, smooth strokes.

"Flower of the Winds, after the compass rose."

"Ah, the windrose . . . the pathway of the lost," he said, glancing at me with a light in his eyes. "I have often seen the figure in old navigation charts."

"For me, there was almost a kind of magic in the name. I remember times when we were out on the boat and the fog would roll in. I'd be terrified of getting lost, but Grandpa Hugh would tell me not to worry—the *Flower of the Winds* would guide us safely home—and she always did."

Sergei turned the bell in his hands so that its newly-polished surface gleamed in the sunlight. *"Ocin krasivi,"* he said with satisfaction. "Very handsome."

I nodded, my mind framing the sight of his strong hands for memory's keeping.

Outside, a chorus of robins was interrupted by the sound of an engine and the crunch of tires moving down the gravel drive.

Sergei's back stiffened, and I glanced out the window to see a tan compact car pull up beside my Honda Civic.

"What does Dr. Harrison look like?"

"Sandy brown hair and beard, both graying. Medium height. He also wears glasses and a bewildered expression."

I smiled slightly at the description, then turned to Sergei. "He's here."

Sergei got to his feet and moved beside me, careful to stand well away from the window. "What will you say to him?"

I shook my head and answered honestly, "I don't know."

We faced each other in silence, then he gave me a brief nod. "I will rely on your judgment."

I could feel the tension building inside me as we left the room. There was so much at stake. What if my judgment weren't good enough?

Sergei paused on the stairs to look at me. "Your eyes, *Kasenya*. The worry is back."

I lowered my gaze, wondering if all my emotions were so transparent to him.

"If it will be of any use, remember this," he said, tilting my chin with a gentle hand. "Dr. Harrison also has many worries. Chances are, he will not notice yours. But one of your smiles would do much to improve his day."

Bill Harrison looked as if his day couldn't get much worse. His sandy brows were drawn together in a tight frown, and he was trudging down the walk as if there were a hundred pound weight on his shoulders.

"You must be Dr. Harrison," I said, offering him a smile. "The Coast Guard told me you'd be coming by. I'm Cassandra Graves."

The man managed a half-hearted nod and shoved his wire-rimmed glasses back on his nose. "I'm sorry to bother you, Miss Graves. One of the crewmen told me your place has steps going down to the beach."

"That's right, but I'm afraid they won't do you any good right now. The tide's in so you won't be able to get around the point. You can see the boat from the back of my place though."

Bill Harrison followed me along the narrow walk leading to the seaward side of the property. Here, a sturdy chain link fence stood as a barrier between the cliff's edge and the hundred foot drop below. Over the years, a natural hedge of salal had completely overgrown the fence. Beside this woodsy camouflage, Grandpa Hugh had placed a redwood bench and clay pots full of showy red geraniums. It was one of my favorite places to watch the sea.

Now, it was Bill Harrison who leaned against the fence and

stared offshore.

"Have the Coast Guard found any survivors?" he asked quietly.

"No. I'm sorry."

His body tensed, then sagged. Behind the glasses, his eyes were bleak.

"One of the crewmen said something about your boat being stolen," I ventured.

He shook his head. "No . . . no, I think some friends may have borrowed it."

"I'm sorry," I said again, wishing I could tell him those friends had not drowned but were safe in the house behind him.

"I'd been having a little engine trouble with her now and then," he mumbled, more to himself than me. "I should've taken her in and had it checked. This is all my fault —" He cleared his throat, then looked out to sea where breakers were crashing around the rocks which imprisoned his boat.

The grief in his eyes helped confirm my decision. I had to tell him. "Would you like to come inside for a few minutes? One of the crewmen said you needed to call and give permission before they could do anything."

Bill Harrison turned away from the fence with a sigh. "I guess so. But right now I don't care what happens to the damn thing."

He's going to help, I thought, feeling a surge of hope as we walked back to the house. Everything's going to be all right.

"Hello, there! I'm glad I caught you. I knocked but didn't get an answer."

Glancing ahead, I saw a man standing on the front steps of the cottage and fear gripped my insides. Kevin! What on earth was he doing here? The next moment, relief replaced the fear, and my knees went weak. The man was about Kevin's height, with the same athletic build and light brown hair, but older, somewhere in his mid-thirties. His blue oxford shirt was open at the throat and rolled up at the sleeves, revealing the kind of tan one sees on California beaches. Dark glasses hid his eyes.

I received a perfunctory nod before the man turned his attention to Dr. Harrison. "Jeff Lloyd, *San Francisco Tribune,*" he said, offering an outstretched hand. "And I'm hoping you're Bill Harrison from OSU."

The professor responded with a cautious nod, and I felt my relief stiffen into wary alertness.

"I'm sure you must be wondering why I'm here and how I know you," the journalist went on, casually withdrawing his hand to remove the sunglasses. "I was at the Coast Guard Station in Newport this morning when the report came in about your boat."

"I can't imagine why my boat should be of such interest to a reporter from San Francisco."

Jeff Lloyd acknowledged this with an easy laugh and slipped the dark glasses over his slicked back hair. "You're right, it isn't the boat so much as its passengers that interests me. I was sent to cover Nikolai Petrovsky's lecture for the Oceanographic Institute, and when word got out he was missing, the paper flew me up to Newport." His cool blue eyes regarded Dr. Harrison with unblinking interest. "Rumor has it, you aided in their defection. At least, that's what Soviet officials are claiming."

"According to my knowledge, there has been no defection," Bill Harrison answered evenly. "As for Nikolai Petrovsky's disappearance, I'm as concerned as the Consulate—perhaps more so, since he was my friend."

"You said *was*. Does that mean you believe Petrovsky and his assistant were using your boat to escape? I understand the Coast Guard don't expect to find any survivors."

Dr. Harrison's face was drawn, his voice colorless. "I'm sorry, Mr. Lloyd, but I have no information for you." Turning to me, he added, "Thank you for your help, Miss Graves."

I had been standing frozen during their conversation. Now, as he turned to go, panic spurred me into action. "But . . . I thought you were going to phone the Coast Guard. . . ."

"There's no need to trouble you any further. I have to drive over to Garibaldi anyway."

Jeff Lloyd stepped in front of Dr. Harrison, blocking his path. "If I could ask just one more question. . . ."

"I'm sorry, but I don't —"

"Since you were a friend of Petrovsky's and Alexandrov," the journalist went on, "I'd be interested in your reaction to the alleged murder charges being brought against them."

I caught my breath at his words.

Bill Harrison's face was a fixed, cold mask. "I have no comment. Now if you'll excuse me. . . ."

"No comment?" Jeff Lloyd echoed, a cynical twist to his mouth. "An attractive woman is found strangled in the Russians' apartment—nude, in Alexandrov's bed—and you have no comment? What about the rumor that he and Ivanova were having an affair?"

"Yelena. . . ." The name came from my lips in a dry whisper as the ground swung up to meet me.

"Miss Graves . . . are you all right?"

Dr. Harrison gripped my arm, and I fought the dizziness with some deep breaths.

"I . . . I'm fine. . . ."

"Are you sure you're all right?"

Something in Jeff Lloyd's voice cut through the sick haze of shock, and I glanced up to find his interested blue eyes on my face.

"Yes . . . for a moment, I didn't feel well . . . that's all."

"Maybe you ought to lie down for a while," Dr. Harrison suggested. "You do look pale. . . ." He gave me a half-hearted smile before turning away. "And don't worry about that phone call. I'll just drive over to Garibaldi."

This time Jeff Lloyd made no move to stop him. "Is there anything I can do?" he asked, turning to me with a look of concern. "I'll be glad to call a doctor."

"No . . . really. I'm much better," I insisted, heading across the lawn toward the drive.

"Hold on a minute. I thought you were going inside to lie down."

I reached the back of the house in time to see Dr. Harrison's car disappear up the wooded drive. "I will . . . I just need a little fresh air."

"You're sure there's no one I can call to give you a hand?"

"No, there's no one to call. Please, don't let me keep you, Mr. Lloyd."

The man hesitated, obviously not convinced. "I hope you don't think I'm being a pest, but I hate to leave—especially if you're here alone. I guess I feel partly responsible. I couldn't help noticing your reaction when I asked Harrison about the woman's murder. I'm sorry if I upset you."

I glanced away from his probing blue eyes, feeling an uncomfortable, nagging worry. Common sense, let alone the devastating facts he had revealed, ought to have me begging him to stay or call the police. Yet something else fought to believe Sergei was innocent, that it was all a mistake.

The sound of a car diverted Jeff Lloyd's attention, and we both glanced toward the drive. For a moment, I thought it might be Dr. Harrison returning, then Mrs. Davis' light blue Chevy appeared out of the trees. The woman gave me a cheery wave as she parked beside the carport.

"You don't need to worry about me any longer," I said, going to meet her. "Mrs. Davis is one of my neighbors."

"Well, well . . . more surprise visitors?" Mrs. Davis asked, getting out of her car.

"Surprise visitors?" came the interested voice beside me.

My heart constricted in a tight knot, but I pretended not to have heard his question. "Hello, Mrs. Davis. Any more news from the Coast Guard?"

"No, dear. I was wondering if you'd found out anything."

"Not a thing."

The journalist answered Mrs. Davis' curious look with a pleasant smile. "Jeff Lloyd, of the *San Francisco Tribune.*"

"You're a reporter?"

"Yes, ma'am."

"Don't tell me—I'll bet you're here to do a story on that boat in the rocks! Did Cassie tell you I was the one who discovered it this morning? Actually, my husband noticed it first, but I called the Coast Guard."

"Is that so?"

I backed away from them with a casual smile. "If you'll excuse me, I'll let Mrs. Davis fill you in on all the details."

"Wait a minute, Cassie! Before you go, I want to give you a special treat I baked for your young man." She turned back to her car and leaned over to retrieve something from the front seat. "I hope Kevin and Mr. Barlow like blueberry pie," she said, proudly presenting me with the pie.

"Thank you. I — I'm sure they will."

"Where is your young man?" she asked, glancing around.

"Well, he's not here right now. They had some business to attend to, but . . . they'll be back later."

"Mrs. Davis, if you have a few minutes, there are some questions I'd like to ask you," Jeff Lloyd said pleasantly.

"Certainly. Are you writing an article?"

He nodded and took her arm. "Would you mind giving me a ride back to my car. It's parked down the road."

"Not at all. I'd be happy to."

Jeff Lloyd gave me a parting smile over his shoulder. "Thanks for your time . . . Cassie, was it? And I hope you're feeling better."

I watched numbly as he helped the woman into her car, then walked swiftly around the front to climb in the passenger side. Beaming with self-importance, Muriel Davis started the engine, backed the car around, and after tossing me a triumphant little wave, headed up the drive.

Chapter 7

I STOOD AFTER they had gone, staring at the sway of cedar trees along the drive, listening to the wind's restless moan through the branches. *Say what people expect you to say. Do what you see others do, and keep your thoughts to yourself.* The significance of Sergei's words shivered through me, more penetrating than the breeze off the ocean. Is that what he and Nikolai were doing—telling me what I wanted to hear in order to gain my confidence and withholding the rest . . . like Yelena's murder?

I hesitated on the porch steps, unable to argue away my doubts and fears. Facts warred with feelings, and the facts left me cold.

I opened the back door and shut it softly behind me. It still wasn't too late to call the police. Sergei and Nikolai would never have to know that I had found out about Yelena's murder.

"*Kasenya. . . ?*"

I jumped at the sound of Sergei's voice and nearly dropped the pie.

He stood near the kitchen table, dark eyes intent on my face, a frown narrowing his brows. "*Kasenya* . . . what has happened?"

Even if I could have found the words, my throat was too dry and constricted to utter a sound.

"Something has frightened you. . . ."

When he stepped toward me, I backed against the door with a gasp, clutching the pie against me. Sergei muttered something in Russian, his dark eyes puzzled by my response.

"I think Cassandra may have bad news for us," Nikolai said,

coming into the room. His canny gaze took in my rigid position against the door and Sergei's hurt expression. "Could we all sit down?" he suggested, "for I have some bad news as well."

When I didn't move, Nikolai gave me a brief nod and walked slowly to the table. "Perhaps if we share this bad news together, it will not seem so hard," he said, sitting down with a heavy sigh. "During your absence, Sergei and I took the liberty of listening to the radio in your grandfather's room. We hoped to learn something of our government's response to our disappearance. . . ." He paused, hazel eyes intent on my face. "Forgive me, but I do not know of a kind or pleasant way to tell you this. Yelena Ivanova is dead. She was found in our apartment last night. And if one is to believe the news reports, Sergei and I are the prime suspects."

"Not *you*," Sergei corrected bitterly. "Do not attempt to shield me, *Kolya*. I am the one accused of this crime. Yelena was found in my bed . . . not yours."

Something in his words and voice eased the tight knot of fear inside me and my legs went weak. "I know."

Sergei stared at me in stunned silence.

"Bill Harrison . . . was it he who told you?" Nikolai asked.

"No, but he knows about the murder. We were talking when a reporter from San Francisco showed up."

"A reporter . . . ?" The professor leaned forward with wary interest. "Did he give you his name?"

"Jeff Lloyd."

"And identification?"

"I — I didn't think to ask. . . ."

"Was he American?"

"Yes."

"You are sure of this?"

I thought of Jeff Lloyd's confident smile, his California tan and brash, almost insolent manner. "Yes, I'm sure."

"Forgive an old man his suspicions," he said, "but the Soviet Consulate is also in San Francisco."

More than suspicions, I thought, seeing the sharp look of fear in his eyes.

"This Mr. Lloyd," Nikolai went on, "did he question you?"

"No. He was more interested in Dr. Harrison. Lloyd seems to think he helped you defect. At least he said that's what the Soviets believe."

Dr. Petrovsky rested one arm on the table with a grieved sigh.

"And what do you believe?" Sergei asked quietly.

I was reluctant to meet his eyes, knowing the question had nothing to do with their defection or Dr. Harrison.

In the silence which followed, Sergei crossed to the wall phone and lifted the receiver off the hook. "Call your police," he said, holding the receiver out to me. "If it will take the fear from your eyes, call them! I will not stop you."

I shook my head, blinking away hot, sudden tears. "I'm afraid for you, *Seriozha*, not me! It's not safe to stay here . . . not now."

Sergei slowly hung up the phone. "Why do you say not now?"

"Because I made a mistake. I lied to him—to Jeff Lloyd—and to Mrs. Davis. . . ."

"Mrs. Davis?" Nikolai broke in. "She was also here?"

I nodded miserably, biting down on my lower lip to stop its trembling.

"I am not sure why this is a problem," he said, "but perhaps if you would care to sit down. . . ?"

Sergei took the pie from me, set it on the counter, then clasped my hands in his. There was strength in his touch. Strength and warmth I could cling to. "Now tell me about this lie," he said calmly.

"I let Jeff Lloyd think I was here alone. He wanted to call someone to help me, but naturally, I didn't want him to come inside, so —"

"One moment," Sergei interrupted. "Why did this reporter wish to get help? Are you ill?"

"No. I'm fine now, but when he was telling Dr. Harrison about Yelena's murder—well, my reaction was pretty strong."

"Stronger than it should have been for someone unacquainted with the situation," Nikolai stated matter-of-factly.

I nodded. "After Dr. Harrison left, I thought the reporter would go, too, but he said he wanted to make sure I was all right. That's when he offered to call someone to help me, and I told him there was no one to call. Then Mrs. Davis showed up with a pie for my young man and his father. . . ."

Sergei's dark brows lifted. "Ah, and suddenly he knows you are not alone."

"I didn't know what else to do. Mrs. Davis asked where you were, and I tried to cover by saying you'd gone out for a while, but I don't know how convincing I was. . . ."

He gave me a close look. "There is something else which troubles you."

"It might be nothing, but Jeff Lloyd left with Mrs. Davis right after that. He said he wanted to ask her a few questions and of course, she was only too eager." I drew a tense breath. "Maybe all he wanted was to interview her about the boat, but I can't help worrying. . . . I'm afraid I've made things worse."

"There is no cause to blame yourself," Nikolai told me. "In any case, the situation is out of our hands. Yelena's death has changed all that." There was resigned hopelessness in his eyes and voice. "Whatever happens, I wish you to remember that you have my gratitude always."

Sergei let go my hands to face his friend. "What are you saying? That you no longer wish political asylum? That you want to go back. . . ?"

"What I wish, what I want . . . it is too late for that, don't you see? The American government will never grant asylum to a criminal. And that is what we are in their eyes. Criminals." He shook his head. "Poor Yelena. Telling you about my arrest was a serious mistake, but I doubt even she imagined the price would be so high. The KGB has moved quickly to get me back." Nikolai sighed and looked at me. "Perhaps Sergei is right after all, about calling your police. And when you tell them about us, you might say we threatened you or used force—that way things should not go too badly for you. . . ."

"I have a better idea," I told him. "I think we should leave now—get you out of here before Mrs. Davis or some other reporter shows up with more questions."

"My dear, have you not understood what I am saying? Your government will not grant. . . ."

"I understand you very well. But in this country, a man is innocent until he's proved guilty. You and Sergei were in Newport all morning; that can be verified. And you took the boat when—around two o'clock?—so there are witnesses who saw you at the Coast Guard station. And I can prove you were here all last night. Don't you see? When the police determine the approximate time Yelena was killed, you'll be cleared. But you're going to need help—a good lawyer and someone like your friend, Paul Miklos."

"Even if what you say is true, how can this help us now?" Nikolai asked me. "Paul Miklos will not return until Monday, and I do not know any lawyers—good or bad."

"Well, I do. Kevin's father is an excellent attorney, and I know if I talk to him. . . . Nevermind, that isn't important right now. The first thing we need to do is get you both out of here."

Sergei faced me in frustration. "You say leave, but to where?"

I smiled at him. "My sister Charlotte has a home a few miles outside Tillamook. It's totally secluded—nothing but pastures and farms for miles. I don't know why I didn't think of it sooner."

"But your sister—won't she object?"

"She and Mark and their boys left this morning on vacation. They'll be gone for almost two weeks. Charlotte called me last night to ask if I'd check on the house and water her plants. It'll be perfect. What do you say?"

He didn't say anything. Instead, I found myself pulled close against his chest in an embrace that took my breath away. The next moment he released me and stepped back with the formal stiffness I was coming to know.

Dr. Petrovsky got to his feet and smiled wryly. "Since everything seems to be decided, perhaps one of you will be kind enough to tell me how we are to be smuggled to your sister's home."

"Don't worry," I said, my emotions still reeling from the hard warmth of Sergei's embrace. "I'll figure out something."

Nikolai patted my shoulder, and I saw the brightness of unshed tears in his eyes. "I'm sure you will, my dear. I'm sure you will."

As it happened, very little smuggling was necessary. In fact, there was a decided lack of drama in our departure. I took the time to grab my grandfather's bathrobe and pajamas, thinking anything else the men might need we could either buy or borrow from my brother-in-law. We left Gulliver in the utility room, contentedly downing another can of tuna fish, then locked the house.

The concealing slope of the hillside and heavy cover of trees made it next to impossible for anyone to see us. Even so, Sergei kept a watchful eye on the driveway while the professor climbed into the Honda's back seat. There was just enough room for him to stretch out comfortably, and I felt reasonably sure his presence would go undetected. Trying to conceal Sergei's tall frame in the front seat of a Honda Civic was another matter. After adjusting the bucket seat as far back as it would go, he was finally able to crouch down on the floor, with his long legs crammed in the limited floor space under the dash and his upper body leaning forward over the seat.

"I'm afraid you're going to be awfully stiff by the time we get there," I said, thinking of the half-hour plus drive to my sister's house.

"If someone should be watching, it is important that you appear to be leaving alone. Later, when we are well away from here, it will not matter so much if I am seen."

Who's going to be watching? I wondered, but didn't dare give voice to the question. The grave expression on Sergei's face was reason enough to accept the possibility.

At the top of the drive, I braked and glanced cautiously in both directions. A short distance down the road, a silver-gray sports car was parked on the shoulder with its hood up. I assumed the owner must have gone for help, because there was no one in sight. And no traffic coming either way. Relieved, I turned left and accelerated.

Traffic was sparse along the mountainous stretch of road between Cape Meares and Bay Ocean. The occupants of the few cars and campers which passed by were more interested in the sparkling glimpses of sea and lush forests than a young woman in a blue-gray Honda. At one point, we were followed by a sleek mini-van with a California plate, but it turned off at Cape Meares State Park. My hopes for Sergei and the professor's safety grew warmer with every mile.

As we drove down a long, gentle hill with shady avenues of alders on either side, I saw the blue waters of Cape Meares Lake straight ahead and the small junction where the Three Capes Loop joined Bay Ocean Road. I slowed to a stop, gave a passing glance to a fisherman casting his line, then turned to Sergei.

"If you want to sit up and stretch your legs, I think its safe to —" A flash of sunlight glinting off metallic gray drew my attention to the rearview mirror where I saw a sports car just cresting the hill behind us. Instinctively, I reached over and shoved Sergei's head and shoulders back down, then hit the gas pedal.

The tires squealed as I made a sharp right turn, and Sergei grabbed onto the seat to steady himself.

"What is wrong?"

"Probably nothing."

"Are we being followed?"

"I'm not sure, but you'd better stay out of sight till we're around the Bay."

Chances were highly unlikely the gray car I'd seen moments ago was the same one parked below Winwood Cottage. We'd already driven several miles without any evidence of being followed. I gave the rearview mirror another quick glance. Nothing. I took some deep breaths, trying to ease the tight knot of tension inside me and concentrated on the road ahead.

Situated between a steep, forested hillside and the water's edge, Bay Ocean Road was not the route to take for someone in a hurry. Especially when the tide was running high, like today. The road's winding course followed every curve of the bay and in places, the water level was nearly as high as the asphalt, with only a narrow ribbon of grassy shoreline separating the two.

I shifted down to maneuver a tight curve and tried to relax my grip on the wheel. To my left, black cormorants bobbed in the shallows. Perched on a half-submerged stump, a kingfisher surveyed his watery domain, his blue-crested head cocked in alertness for the sight of fish below the surface.

Not far ahead, a pick-up truck pulling a boat and trailer was backing across the road onto a narrow shoulder. I slowed to give him ample room and caught a brief glimpse of silver behind me.

The next moment, dense foliage and the overhanging walls of the cliff blocked my view. For the next mile or so, I made frequent checks in the mirror, but the curving road prevented me from seeing more than a short distance.

"Someone is following," Sergei said, his quiet words a statement of fact rather than a question.

"A few minutes ago I noticed a gray car behind us."

"And this gives you concern?"

"When we first pulled out of the driveway, there was a silver-gray Porsche parked down the road with its hood up."

"Is anyone following now?"

"I can't see far enough behind us to be sure. Once we get around the bay, the road straightens out and—it's still there! Just before we came around that last curve, I saw him. . . ."

Sergei's voice was even and calm. "Drive normally, *Kasenya*, at your usual speed."

I relaxed my fierce hold on the wheel and tried to do as he said. Two minutes passed in taut silence.

"When you have a clear view of the road behind us, slow down," he instructed, "but only slightly."

Keeping one eye on the rearview mirror, I did as he asked. Seconds later, a metallic gleam appeared from around a heavily-wooded bend, then quickly pulled back.

My voice was dry. "He's still there."

"You are doing very well, *Kasenya*. Maintain a regular speed now, as if you were not aware anyone is following."

The gears groaned as my foot slipped off the clutch. "Sorry, I guess I'm a little shaky."

Sergei said nothing, but for a moment, I felt the comforting pressure of his hand on my knee.

Another mile passed by and the road left the bay to cut through the gentle pastures of a dairy farm. It wouldn't be long before we reached the junction where Bay Ocean Road joined the main highway leading to Tillamook. Somehow, I had to lose the Porsche before we turned north onto '101.'

A cautious glance in the mirror assured me the gray sports car was still keeping well behind us. I fought the temptation to press on the gas and tried to think. I might be able to lose him on a side street in Tillamook, but it was risky at best.

About a hundred yards ahead, the junction came into view. Beyond that, a narrow bridge spanned the Tillamook River.

I gripped the wheel with sudden determination and hit the gas pedal. "Hang on. I have an idea."

"An idea — ?"

The Honda reached fifty in seconds. I slowed just long enough to check traffic beyond the junction, then cruised through the stop sign and roared toward the bridge. The summer before, a fire had destroyed the old wooden pilings which supported the bridge, and construction crews were replacing them with concrete. As recent as four months ago, traffic across the bridge was still one-way, with a traffic light on either side to regulate the flow. Locals had groaned and moaned about the delays, but now I found myself praying the light was still there.

It was. The green changed to red moments before I got there, but I gunned the gas pedal and kept on going. Ignoring the angry shouts of the road crew, I bit down on my lower lip and sailed past them, barely clearing the bridge before the line of cars on the opposite side started through.

A quick glance in the rearview mirror produced the distinctive finger gesture of a burly young man in bib overalls—but no silver-gray Porsche. By the time traffic was through and the light changed again, I should have at least a full minute's head start. One minute. To get off the main highway and out of sight.

The Honda sang along at sixty, then sixty-five, while I prayed that all of Tillamook's finest would be occupied somewhere at the other end of town.

"*Kasenya* . . . what are you — ?"

"It's all right," I told him, racing past another dairy farm where brown and white Guernseys were grazing in the fields. "I know what I'm doing."

The hospital was located in a residential section of town, just outside the business district. I dropped speed sharply when it came into view, passed by at the regulation speed, then turned left onto a small side street. A few blocks later, I turned right. Keeping to the backstreets, I was able to miss the business section of Tillamook altogether and entered Highway 101 near the railroad tracks north of town.

Afternoon traffic was fairly congested, with a steady stream of diesels, cars and an occasional logging truck, but I drove for three full minutes without any sign of the silver-gray Porsche.

"You can sit up now," I told Sergei with a relieved sigh. "I'm pretty sure we've lost him."

Sergei shifted his body around on the seat, then stretched his long legs in front of him. Smiling, he said something to me in Russian. It sounded so wonderful I hated to ask for a translation, half afraid it might be, "How much longer before we get to your sister's house," or "Could we stop at a gas station?"

"My feelings exactly," came a voice from the back seat. "Although I must confess, I lack your poetic fire."

I glanced over my shoulder to see the professor grinning broadly at the two of us.

"Are you all right?" I asked, realizing with some embarrassment that I'd completely forgotten about the man.

"Fine, fine," he answered, then leaned forward to give Sergei a meaningful tap on the shoulder. "Aren't you going to give Cassandra a translation?"

Sergei shrugged. "In English, the words are not the same," he answered shortly, then turned to me. "How long before we reach the house of your sister?"

"Not long—only a few miles," I answered, telling myself there was no reason to feel disappointed. But inside I couldn't help wondering if I would ever hear a translation of *Seriozha's* "poetic fire."

Chapter 8

WHEN I TURNED off Highway 101 to take the Kilchis River road, the only vehicle following us was a battered blue pick-up truck. Before long, it turned onto a rutted lane leading to a dairy farm. For the first time since we had left Winwood Cottage, I felt myself beginning to relax.

The afternoon was sunny and the breeze blowing through the car windows was a heady mixture of sweet clover, warm hay and dairy cows. I glanced sideways to see Sergei taking in the calm landscape, his right arm resting on the door frame, the wind teasing a few strands of dark hair across his forehead.

"What is the name for this river?" he asked, pointing to the lazy sparkle of blue running through lush pastures and wooded glens.

"Kilchis."

"Kil-chees," he repeated. "This is Indian name?"

I nodded. "Take away the houses and farms, and the area probably wouldn't look much different than it did when the Tillamooks lived here."

"I like this Kil-chees place," he said, turning his face to the breeze. "It has a peaceful atmosphere."

"My brother-in-law feels the same way," I told him with a smile. "Mark's always bragging to his friends at the office that he has more cows than people for neighbors."

I left the Kilchis River road and turned onto a narrow country lane where the grass growing on either side was nearly as high as the Honda. After crossing an old wooden bridge, we wound our way through varying shades of green, toward a forested knoll. On the crest of the hill, set among a stand of firs and spruces, was a large home with twin gables of dark timber.

"That's Charlotte and Mark's place straight ahead," I said, adding as we passed two small frame houses, "I don't think we'll need to worry about the neighbors. I'm sure Charlotte's already told them I'll be checking on the house."

Sergei only nodded and said nothing.

I parked the Honda on the circular drive in front of the house, grateful that both the garage and main entrance faced away from the road and were well-shielded by the evergreens. Only two days ago, the location of an entrance would never have entered my mind.

Sergei gave me a curious glance as I approached a wooden barrel brimming over with nasturtiums and picked up a large ceramic goose nesting in the midst of the flowers. His dark eyes widened even more when I retrieved the garage door opener, gave it two clicks and the door went up with a shuddering groan.

The men followed without a word as I led them through the garage into the kitchen. Even in winter, when gray clouds refused to allow the sun's shining, Charlotte's kitchen was a cheerful place to be. Cinnamon and nutmeg-colored curtains, fringed with creamy vanilla lace, framed a large bay window above an old-fashioned window seat. There were always flowers on the big oak table, samples of the boys' artwork proudly displayed on the refrigerator and treats in the cookie jar.

"If you like, I can show you through the house now, then we'll have lunch," I said, heading for the entryway.

Sergei and the professor hesitated in the front hall, silently taking in the spacious living room with its vaulted ceilings, carved oak mantle and Charlotte's unique style of country decorating. If three woven baskets looked good, six would be even better, was her motto. That same principle applied to pillows, potted plants, and her latest fad—ceramic ducks and geese. Their black eyes and painted orange bills were everywhere, peeping out among the pothos and dried flower arrangements, waddling across the hearth, even posing on the lamp tables beside pictures of the children.

Nikolai gave me a faint smile and said, "Charming," as we headed for the staircase, but I sensed he was ill at ease.

The men seemed even more uncomfortable after glimpsing Mark and Charlotte's huge master bedroom with its four-poster bed, walk-in closets and private bath.

"The boys' rooms are down the hall," I said hurriedly. "Brian's into baseball right now, and Peter's a real dinosaur nut."

Nikolai glanced into my nephew's bedroom with its fearsome displays of prehistoric life and gave me a weary smile. "Right now, I believe I would feel more at home with the dinosaurs."

His smile couldn't disguise the sadness in his voice and suddenly I understood their silence. These men had no home, no possessions, nothing that was familiar with the touch of belonging. Winwood Cottage, with its simple furnishings and feel of the sea, had been a refuge, a haven. But now they were thrust into a stranger's home in his absence, a home that fairly shouted with the presence of money and material ease.

"I think you'd like Peter," I told the professor as we headed back toward the stairs. "He loves books and he's the only four-year-old I know who can pronounce pteradactyl."

"I hope one day we shall have the pleasure of meeting each other," he responded politely, but without any real conviction.

I wanted to tell him, "Of course you will," but the uncertainty of the days ahead made me hesitate. Instead, I went on a shade too brightly, "I'll bet you both must be starving. Just make yourselves at home, and I'll fix us some lunch."

Charlotte had done an excellent job of making sure no food would spoil while they were away. Except for a few condiments and canned drinks, the refrigerator was empty. A search of the cupboards produced some canned goods, mostly soup and tuna fish. For once, even the cookie jar was empty.

We sat down to chicken noodle soup, saltine crackers and soft drinks. Looking at the men's solemn faces, I realized the menu was hardly a primary concern. I could have served prime rib and they probably wouldn't have noticed.

"I'm sorry there isn't more for lunch," I said, trying to fill the silence. "Since you'll be here over the weekend, I'd better go into

Tillamook this afternoon and do some grocery shopping."

Sergei glanced up with a frown. "Later, when we are established, you will be fully repaid."

"It's only some groceries. . . ."

"If you will please keep the receipt, I will take care of it," he said firmly.

I gave in with a shrug. "All right, but we don't need to worry about that now. Is there anything special you'd like for dinner? I'm not the greatest cook, but I —"

"So many choices," Nikolai interrupted with a frustrated sigh. "What clothes to wear . . . what food to eat . . . always I am making a choice."

Sergei put a hand on the older man's arm. "You are weary, Kolya."

The professor only shrugged and stared out the window.

Looking at the pallor of his skin, I couldn't help thinking he might be ill as well as tired and made a mental note to add cough drops and cold medicine to my shopping list.

"There are some books and magazines in the family room if you'd like to read for awhile," I offered. "And there's always television. Charlotte and Mark have a whole shelf full of video cassettes —" I broke off, realizing I was throwing the poor man still another round of choices.

I got up from the table and took my dishes to the sink. "Well, I guess I'd better get the shopping done. I'll be gone about an hour," I told Sergei, forcing a cheerfulness I didn't feel. "And don't worry about dinner. I'll surprise you. . . ."

I never imagined shopping at Safeways could be filled with such intrigue. Before entering the store, I gave the parking lot a thorough once-over, but there were no Porsche's to be seen, silver or otherwise. Wandering up and down the aisles, I felt alternately foolish and frightened, wondering if anyone were watching me. And as the checker rang up my purchases, I smiled and thought, if I were to tell you who would be using these groceries, it would wipe that bored look right off your face.

Driving back to Charlotte's, I glanced at my wristwatch and my pleasure in the afternoon's shopping promptly faded. I'd told Sergei I would be gone one hour, and over two had passed since I'd left. Naturally, because I was in a hurry, the traffic was heavy and sluggish. It seemed forever before I turned onto the Kilchis River road, and then I was stopped by a large herd of holsteins, ambling across the road for evening milking. By the time I pulled into the garage, it was going on six.

I hurried into the kitchen with a grocery sack under each arm and met the men's worried frowns. "I'm sorry I'm late. I wasn't keeping track of the time and. . . ."

"You were not followed?" Sergei asked shortly.

"No. Everything's fine," I assured him, setting the sacks on the table.

"There were no difficulties with the car?" he asked next, and the coldness in his voice made me cringe.

"Nothing's wrong with the car. It's just—everything took longer than I thought. I had to stop and get gas, and then I thought you might want today's newspaper, so I went back for one." When he didn't say anything, I added lamely, "I probably shouldn't have taken the time to stop at the video store, but. . . ."

"Video store!" he burst out.

"Seriozha, as you can see, Kasenya is fine," Nikolai inserted mildly. "There is no reason to alarm yourself."

Sergei ignored him and turned to me. "Excuse my lack of understanding. I was afraid some harm may have come to you. How could I forget the great obsession you Americans have to be entertained."

I gave him a frosty look, then stalked out of the kitchen to get the rest of the groceries with both men following.

"What is all this?" Nikolai asked, as I picked up a sack from the front seat of the car. "So much, Cassandra. . . ."

Ignoring Sergei, I gave the professor an especially warm smile and handed him the groceries. "Tillamook cheese, smoked sausage and another American obsession—ice cream. I thought you might enjoy some for dessert, so I stopped at the Cheese Factory."

I bent down for the remaining sack, along with a small plastic bag containing the videos. "These are for you," I said, thrusting the videos at Sergei, then slamming the car door.

A puzzled look replaced his anger as he removed the cassettes from the bag.

"*Doctor Zhivago . . . chudesnyi!*" Nikolai exclaimed. "I saw parts of this film on my last visit, two years ago. A thoughtful choice, wouldn't you agree, Seriozha?"

For a moment, Sergei's expression was unguarded as he looked into my eyes. "*Spaseba,*" he said softly and bent to kiss my cheek.

We prepared dinner together, and Sergei took delight in teasing me about my 'international' menu.

"Swiss cheese, crackers from the English, French bread and Italian spaghetti," he said, looking over the table. "Where is representative from mother Russia?"

"I couldn't find any cavier, so this'll have to do."

He caught the bottle I tossed him and laughed. "Russian dressing . . . very good."

Nikolai came into the kitchen then, shaking the newspaper and muttering an angry stream of Russian. "When will American media learn to take the wool from its eyes?" he stormed. "When will they recognize the difference between reporting of facts and *provokatsiya!*"

I left the pot of boiling noodles to face him. "What's wrong?"

"*Provokatsiya!*" he repeated, tossing the newspaper on the table in disgust. "A KGB plot!"

Sergei picked up the paper, and his face tightened with anger as he scanned the article.

"If one is to believe what is printed here," Nikolai told me, "Sergei is a spy hired by your CIA to lure me away from Soviet Union. Yelena found out about Sergei's covert activities, and for this she was killed."

I stared at him. "That's crazy! What kind of proof do they have for making such a wild statement?"

"Ah, there is a letter," Nikolai informed me, irony lacing his tone. "A love letter written by Yelena, in which she expresses her great shock and sorrow over his spying. It also states she can no longer remain silent, no matter how much she loves him."

I left the stove to stand beside Sergei. "Do you think there really is such a letter?"

"I am sure there is," Nikolai answered soberly. "The KGB must have forced her to write it . . . before they killed her."

Sergei glanced up from the paper with a frown. "This says our car was found near a place called Monmouth. Where is that?"

"A city north of Corvallis," I told him. "But I thought you said you left the car in Newport."

Sergei nodded. "We did."

"Notice also," the professor pointed out, "that suitcases were found in the car. Suitcases which were in our apartment only yesterday morning."

I glanced over Sergei's shoulder at the newspaper. "Is there any mention of Dr. Harrison or the University?"

"Very little is said about the University, only that we are here on scientific exchange. And there is nothing about Bill Harrison."

"That's strange. After Jeff Lloyd's visit, I expected to see something. Maybe he got wind of the CIA thing and decided that angle was more sensational."

Sergei's expression was thoughtful. "It may be significant rather than strange that the details are so different."

"What do you mean?"

"If authorities are searching for us near this Monmouth area, who then was following today?"

"I don't know, but I'm sure the FBI and police are investigating this. And it won't take much to prove you aren't working for the CIA. I don't care what Yelena's letter says. The whole thing is ridiculous!"

"Perhaps," Nikolai agreed, "but the seed has been planted—printed in black and white for American people to read. Certainly, your government will make their denials, but will it matter? And how many people will believe, especially when CIA's credibility has been damaged by past cover-ups and scandal?" He sat down with a heavy sigh. "And that is what KGB hopes for—to plant those seeds of doubt. It puts your government on the defensive and distracts people from the real problem. If there is one thing a Soviet understands, it is the power of the printed word."

A sick, cold feeling inside told me he was right. "Then Sergei is a scapegoat. The bait to get you back."

Nikolai nodded. "Exactly."

Boiling liquid bubbled and hissed over the sides of the pan, and I hurried over to remove the lid. Stirring the noodles, I gave the clock over the stove a quick glance. "The news is on. Maybe we can find out something more about this."

The information on the television news report was almost identical to that carried by the newspaper. Soviet officials expressed outrage over the disappearance of Nikolai Petrovsky and accused the U.S. government of luring away one of their top scientists. The CIA emphatically denied that Sergei Alexandrov had ever worked for them, and there were no new leads in the murder of Yelena Ivanova. The Soviets also expressed their concern for the safety of Dr. Petrovsky, and both sides pledged full cooperation in the search for the missing Russians. It was not known how the incident would affect upcoming arms negotiations.

Our meal was silent and solemn, certainly not the pleasant occasion I had hoped for. Nikolai didn't touch his salad, ate little of the spaghetti, then excused himself to go lie down. Sergei and I didn't fare much better.

I looked at the table of untouched food with a little sigh and carried the bowl of spaghetti sauce over to the counter.

Sergei got up from the table, watching while I hunted through the drawers for a carton of plastic wrap. "I am sorry that all your preparation did not receive much enjoyment."

I tried to cover my disappointment with a philosophical smile. "Oh, well. At least you'll have plenty of leftovers for tomorrow." I'd been foolish to think we could have a peaceful, pleasant evening together. Foolish and unrealistic. The shopping, the ice cream, the videos. . . . I realized suddenly that all my preparations had been carried out with one motive in mind . . . to please Sergei and

Nikolai. Why not admit it? I'd done it to please Sergei.

Returning to the table for the rest of the dishes, I caught his dark eyes regarding me with interest. I glanced down, giving all my attention to scraping the plates.

"Would you make sure Dr. Petrovsky takes two of those cold tablets tonight? Oh, and I think I left his cough drops on the dresser in Peter's room.'

"You are going?"

"I think it's better if I do. I'll call you sometime tomorrow."

"I do not think it is better for you to go," he said firmly.

My pulse quickened as I turned to face him. "Why not?"

"Are you forgetting Mrs. Davis has seen us? By now, it is quite possible she may know who we are."

"Well, I can't stay away the whole weekend. You're the one who told me I should keep up appearances, do what I normally do . . . and I should be back at the cottage."

"But it may not be safe."

"Why not?" I asked again. "You heard the news. The police are looking for you and Nikolai around Monmouth and Salem."

Sergei reached out and pulled me to him, both hands gripping my shoulders. "That does not mean others will not be searching— or watching closer by. Have you forgotten so soon we were followed today?"

"No, but I—it's possible I was mistaken. . . ."

"You do not believe that, nor do I. What is making you so eager to leave?"

"I'm not eager to leave! I just don't see why I should stay. You and Nikolai will do fine without me. . . ."

Sergei's fierce grip softened, and he gave my shoulders a gentle squeeze. "How can I do fine, as you say, when I am feeling such anxiety for you, *Kasenya?*"

My disappointment in the evening suddenly vanished, and I found myself saying, "Well, maybe I could stay a little longer. . . ."

My words were cut off by the sharp ringing of the phone. I jumped as if the sound had been a rifle shot, and Sergei pulled me close against his chest. We both stared at the phone as it rang again.

"Should I answer it?"

He drew a tight breath, then nodded.

Heart thudding, I moved out of his arms and picked up the receiver. A woman's voice answered my breathless hello with the sharp demand, "Who's this?"

I swallowed hard. "This is Charlotte's sister, Cassandra. Who's calling, please?"

Sergei moved close beside me, leaning his dark head next to the phone, as the woman identified herself as one of Charlotte's neighbor's down the road.

Some of the sharp-edged tension left me, and I was able to say more calmly, "I'm sorry if I worried you, Mrs. Erickson. I assumed Charlotte told you I'd be checking on the house."

"Well, she did say somebody would be by, but when I saw you coming and going today, I wasn't sure if things were all right. If you hadn't answered, I was about set to call the police."

Sergei and I shared a quick look while I reassured the woman that everything was fine. "You'll probably be seeing me on and off during the weekend," I added, thinking I'd better come up with something to justify my presence at the house. "I'm . . . uh, doing some sketches of the boys and thought I'd work on them while Charlotte's away."

Mrs. Erickson was so delighted by this, I was half afraid she would want to see them. Instead, she asked if I would mind checking on her place as well, since she and her husband were driving into Portland to visit relatives for the weekend.

I hung up the phone and turned to Sergei. "Well, that's one less thing you need to worry about. The Erickson's couldn't have picked a better time to go to Portland."

"All of this does not change my worry for you," he said.

Looking into his dark eyes, I was strongly tempted to "forget" about Kevin's phone call and tell Sergei I'd spend the evening. It was nearly ten-thirty in New York. Knowing Kevin, he'd probably called at least once by now and was wondering where I was. I tried to push away a surge of resentment, realizing this was the second time today that a phone call from my fiance had intruded on my time with Sergei.

"I guess I'd better finish putting the food away," I said without much enthusiasm. "Oh, and I'd better leave you my phone number in case you need anything."

"And what if you should need to contact us?" Sergei asked. "Unless we know who is calling, Kolya and I cannot answer."

"You're right. I guess we both need some kind of signal to know who's calling."

Sergei folded his arms across his chest and leaned thoughtfully against the counter. "When you call here, allow two rings and hang up. Then call again. We will do the same."

"Sounds simple enough."

The rest of the food and dishes were cleared away in minutes, and I couldn't think of a legitimate excuse to prolong my stay.

"Well, I guess I'd better go," I said, picking up my car keys and handbag from the counter. "Say goodnight to the professor for me."

"I will."

"And you'll make sure he takes the cold tablets?"

Sergei smiled and nodded.

"If it gets too cold, there are extra blankets in the hall closet upstairs."

"Spaseba."

I half-turned to go. "I forgot to show you how to use the VCR—that is, if you still want to watch the video. . . ."

"I will wait until you can join us. Perhaps tomorrow evening?"

I smiled, feeling like I'd just been asked to my first homecoming dance. "Tomorrow evening. I'll make us a big bowl of popcorn. Do you like popcorn?"

"Very much. With 'tons' of butter," he added in a teasing tone.

The fact he would use my exaggerated expression from the night before filled me with heady warmth.

We stood there smiling at each other until I said again, "I guess I'd better go."

"If I could trouble you with one more request?"

"Of course."

"After your return, will you please call?" Sergei reached out and casually brushed a lock of hair off my shoulder. "It would ease my—our concerns for your safety."

"It's no trouble. I'll be glad to call. Oh, and before I forget, I need to give you my number at the cottage." I set my handbag down and fumbled through its contents for a scrap of paper.

"I was going to indulge in one of your American obsessions," Sergei told me as I scribbled the number on a deposit slip. "If you could stay a few minutes more, it would please me to have your company."

I gave a nervous laugh, seeing a mental image of Kevin dialing the phone in his hotel room. "Which obsession did you have in mind?"

"A dish of ice cream." Sergei took my hand along with the piece of paper and smiled down at me. "Back in Soviet Union, we also have many kinds, but they all taste like vanilla."

I laughed again, amazed that eyes so dark could also be so warm. "I guess a few minutes won't make much difference. . . ."

Chapter 9

A TILTING HALF-MOON seemed to mock me with his silvery, lop-sided grin as I drove back along Bay Ocean Road. Far across the dark stretch of water, the lights of Garibaldi glimmered like earth-bound stars against the black mountainside. Closer by, the distinctive silhouette of a lone heron standing in the tide flats caught my eye. I slowed the car to a stop by the side of the road and switched off the headlights.

Soft night air drifted through the open windows, carrying the scent of wild berries, evergreens and the salty hint of the sea. I turned off the engine, preferring the rhythmic lapping of the bay and a throaty chorus of frogs in the marshes.

By now, Kevin was either frantic or furious. Probably both. It was past two in the morning, New York time, so I really couldn't blame him. He'd never accept the simple explanation that I'd gone out for the evening without a detailed account of where I was, who I was with and what I was doing. And how could I tell Kevin I'd spent the evening eating ice cream and talking with a friend named Sergei? On the surface, it sounded innocent enough. There was nothing wrong with just talking to a friend, but that still didn't explain why I'd stayed out so long. Somehow, I couldn't bring myself to lie and say the time had gotten away, when I knew very well how late it was. Staying with Sergei had been a conscious choice . . . not something that just happened.

I leaned back against the seat, expecting the usual feelings of guilt that came whenever my impulsiveness caused a conflict in our relationship. Instead, I found myself smiling over something Sergei had said and remembering the husky richness of his laugh.

Our conversation had wandered freely throughout the evening, each of us eager to share the separate paths our lives had taken us, and discovering somewhere along the way that we had been travelling parallel paths—miles apart in physical distance, yet, strangely, it was as if we had been walking side by side all the time.

And there were other discoveries. . . .

I closed my eyes, remembering his soft *"do svidaniya, Kasenya . . ."* as we stood next to the car. I had looked up at him, trying to say a casual good-bye and found myself aching to touch the smooth hollows beneath his cheekbones, the slight cleft in his chin. . . .

As if my thoughts were open to him, Sergei had taken my hand, drawn it slowly, deliberately down the side of his face, then pressed a kiss in the center of my palm.

A shivering sigh escaped me as I recalled how his mouth had lingered, melting a warm path straight through me, finding a soft core of pleasure and emotions that had lain untouched until that moment.

I glanced over my shoulder at the moon and sighed again. Oh, Kevin . . . what on earth am I going to tell you?

By the time I reached Winwood Cottage, I had my upcoming conversation well-rehearsed. Without knowing it, Sergei had given me the perfect solution earlier in the day. *If you cannot speak freely, withholding part of the truth is still better than a lie.* And so I would tell Kevin that I'd gone over to Charlotte's to check on the house, then decided to take a drive. Yes, I knew it was late, and I was sorry to worry him, but I had a lot on my mind. Period. If he sulked or complained, there was nothing I could do about it.

After parking the car, I stood for a moment, listening to the rushing voice of the sea, watching the quiet passage of clouds across the face of the moon and knew that my phone call to Kevin would have to wait a few minutes more while I called Sergei to let him know I was back.

A furry shape brushed against my legs as I walked across the lawn, and I glanced down with a start.

"Gulliver! You silly cat." I picked up the tom, enjoying his welcoming purrs. "Are you glad to see me, kitty?"

I took three more steps toward the house, then stopped. Gulliver had been locked inside when we left this afternoon. I was certain all the windows were closed. A sudden shiver raised the flesh on my arms. I was being watched. Someone was inside the house.

"Come on, Gulliver. Let's get my things out of the car. Are you hungry, kitty?" I prattled on, fear making my voice light and breathless, my knees weak as water.

I felt their presence even more strongly when I turned my back to the house. Gulliver must have sensed something as well, because suddenly he growled low in his throat and dug his claws into my arm.

Fear snapped inside me and terror broke loose. I ran back to the car like a wild thing, threw Gulliver inside, and scrambled into the driver's seat. My heart was pounding so loud I couldn't think what I had done with the car keys until I felt their hard metal edge cutting into my hand. Two dark shapes emerged from the house as I jammed the key into the ignition. That same moment I realized the car doors were unlocked and the window on the driver's side half open. It seemed forever before my fingers flipped the locks on the door handles. As I struggled with the window, the dark, running shapes became men with pale faces and long arms, reaching out for the car.

Forgetting the window, I turned the key and the engine sprang to life. Shoving the gears into reverse, I backed out of the carport onto the wet lawn. The tires skidded and spun on the soft ground, as the pale faces came closer.

A fleshy hand grasped the edge of the window, and I saw the hard glimmer of a man's gold ring, then the Honda lurched forward and shot up the drive.

The men lunged after me at a dead run. I turned right without stopping, away from Tillamook and the Kilchis house, down the dark road toward Oceanside.

I had almost a full minute on the lonely road before the flash of headlights appeared in my rearview mirror, moving up fast. Fear struck my chest like a physical blow, and the car responded with a throaty roar as my foot hit the gas. Skidding around curves, shooting past black columns of fir and hemlock, I raced down the mountain. Except for brief, blessed seconds when the winding road ran interference, the glaring white eyes were never far behind.

Shrieking tires competed with Gulliver's frightened yowls as I took a tight curve too fast, then overcorrected with the wheel.

I heard my voice saying, "It's all right, kitty. It's all right," like a mindless recording, as I fought for control of the car.

At Oceanside, I ran the stop sign and swung a hard left, rejecting the steep, one-way streets of the little community for the cliffside road leading to Netarts.

Wisps of ghost fog drifted through the forests. Far below, the curl of the breakers were like pale fingers, crawling toward shore. The next moment, the sea, the forest and the winding road disappeared in a misty blur. Panic tightened my throat, and I slammed on the brakes as the edge of the cliff loomed precariously near. A few heartbeats later, the mist cleared, allowing me a brief glimpse of the road ahead. No turn-offs, no place to hide . . . only dense forests with a few summer homes set back in the trees.

Headlights materialized out of the swirling fog behind me, and I realized my pursuers had the distinct advantage of following my taillights, rather than the road. As the white eyes drew nearer, I had a nightmare vision of my car being forced off the road, plunging down to the sea. I whipped around a tight s-curve, desperation defying caution, then gunned up a short incline. The maneuver added precious seconds to my lead. Cresting the rise, I saw the lights of Netarts straight ahead. I shot forward and raced down the hill with Gulliver yowling protest all the way.

The main street dead-ended near some beach-front motels. I passed by two small grocery stores and a gas station, all closed for the night. Then I glimpsed a narrow side street, half-hidden by overhanging branches of alders and evergreens. Seizing the moment, I made a hard right onto the street and switched off my headlights. Blackness engulfed me, and for the first minute or so, I felt as if I were driving blind. I shifted down, not daring to use brakes or lights for fear they would reveal my presence. Even after my eyes had adjusted to the darkness, the road was difficult to see, cloaked as it was by curling mist and drooping boughs. Patches of moonlight and the occasional light from a summer cottage were my only guides.

After crawling along the hillside for almost a mile, the trees gave way to a grassy slope, and I discovered Netarts Bay lay directly below. A sharp left turn brought me down the slope, where the road opened up into a large parking area near the boat dock and marina. Street lamps and the neon lights of a small cafe brightened the area where two cars and a pick-up truck were parked.

I drove up to the cafe, hoping to find help or a telephone and discovered a dog-eared CLOSED sign in the front window. For no reason other than the fact I couldn't think what to do or where else to go, I pulled into the space between a pick-up truck and a Ford mustang. Gulliver's caterwauling had long since subsided to low yowls of complaint from somewhere under the seat. His pitiful mews and the barking of a dog somewhere on the hillside were the night's only sounds.

I glanced over my shoulder to the dark hillside road. Nothing. Were they searching for me back on the main highway? Or had they given up the chase?

As I sat there, two men sauntered out of the cafe, one bearded and laughing, the other bald and smoking a pipe. The men gave me a brief, passing glance, then climbed into the pick-up truck and backed out. My decision to follow was purely instinctive. I didn't care where they were going. Anything was better than sitting here alone and exposed.

The truck left the marina and turned onto Whiskey Creek Road. From there, it followed the Netarts Highway a short distance before heading north on the road back to Tillamook. I was hoping to follow it all the way into town, but a few miles later, the truck left the highway for a wooded lane leading to a farmhouse, and my sense of isolation returned.

By the time I reached Tillamook, it was half past midnight. The ever present fear of being followed kept me alert and watchful as I drove through town. Strange, how checking the rearview mirror, parked cars and side streets had become almost second nature.

Finally, the lights of Tillamook were behind me, and the Honda was the only car on the Kilchis River road. As I drove past black forests and moonlit fields, a new fear crept into my thoughts. Was *Seriozha* still safe? Reason argued that he was, but my emotions weren't convinced. It was obvious his and Nikolai's presence had been discovered at Winwood Cottage. What if someone had found out about Charlotte's place as well? Words pulsed through my mind like a silent prayer. Please be all right. Please be all right. . . .

The angular shadow of the house was barely visible against the larger blackness of the hillside. I wondered briefly if I should turn off my headlights, then decided it probably didn't matter. If someone were watching, he would have seen the car by now.

The gabled house was black and silent. I pulled onto the circular drive and sat for almost a minute with the engine running, hoping for a feeling—something to let me know all was well. This time there was no ominous sense of danger, no chilling premonition—only the heavy hands of fatigue.

Taking the garage door opener from the glove compartment, I gave it two clicks, then drove the Honda into the space beside Mark's BMW. Another click brought the door back down, shutting out the night and the rest of the world.

I breathed a long sigh. Nothing in the brightly-lit garage seemed disturbed or out of place—the garden tools, the boys' bikes and toys.

Gulliver leaped across my lap the moment I opened the car door and began prowling around the unfamiliar territory.

I let myself quietly into the darkened kitchen, then leaned against the door.

"*Kasenya. . . ?*"

He came toward me through the darkness, and I ran to the haven of his arms. Explanations would come later. Now I could only cling to him, trembling, trying not to cry.

Sergei's arms tightened around me, and I buried my face in the warm hollow of his neck.

"When you didn't call, I knew something had happened. . . ."

His voice, harsh and unsteady, sent the tears I had been struggling to hold back, flowing freely down my face.

"They were waiting . . . inside the cottage."

"Who was waiting?"

I gulped back a sob. "I don't know . . . two men."

He muttered something in Russian, then more gently, "Don't cry, *dushenka*. I have you."

"They didn't follow me here. I promise you, I wasn't followed, or I wouldn't have come back."

"Shhh, we will talk later." He kissed my tear-stained cheeks and smoothed my hair. "When you are feeling better, then you can tell me what happened."

"Don't let me go. . . ."

His lips brushed lightly against mine, then, lifting me effortlessly in his arms, he carried me out of the kitchen.

Moonlight, filtering through lace curtains made shadow roses on the wall beside the living room couch. Black filigree flowers that trembled in the night breeze . . . as I was trembling.

Except for that brief moment in the kitchen, Sergei had not kissed me again. He'd held me close, murmured husky words of comfort I felt rather than understood, and wiped my tears with gentle hands.

Now, cradled in his arms, the danger past, I felt safe as a child who finds comfort after a nightmare. But comfort was no longer enough. That brief taste of his mouth was not enough. Inside, I understood his restraint and the reason for it, but that no longer mattered. Beneath my cheek, I could feel the hard racing of his heart and knew his desires were the same as mine.

I straightened up to face him in the moonlight. His eyes were black and fathomless as they gazed into mine. Although the sea was miles away, I could feel its mystical spell hovering in the air around us. The same compelling force that had drawn me to his side the night before, beckoned and called to me now.

Unable to bear the sweet ache inside me a moment longer, I drew his dark head to mine, seeking and finding the warmth of his mouth.

His touch answered questions that had haunted my dreams for years. Romance did not have to be sacrificed for the sake of reality. Tenderness and passion could be found together. I never imagined I could feel so much . . . give so much.

In his arms, I bid a silent farewell to the Princess Cassandra of my youth. She and Sinbad were welcome to sail away for ports unknown in their ship of dreams. My own dreams had found safe harbor with a man named *Seriozha*. . . .

They returned in the night, long arms with pale hands snaking out of the darkness. I tried to escape them, but my body was leaden, unable to move. Fleshy, grasping fingers groped for my face. I tried to scream, but I had no voice.

"It's all right, *dushenka*. I'm here."

His arms came around me, warm and strong.

I woke, trembling, still feeling the dark presence of the dream.

"I'm here, *dushenka*," he said again, softly kissing my face.

My breath came in frightened gasps as I clutched his hand. "They were after me . . . arms coming out of the darkness. . . ."

"No harm will come to you. It was only a dream." Sergei kissed my cheek and the curve of my neck, then drew the heavy afghan closer around us.

I held him close, needing the warm reassurance of his presence to push the fear away. His kisses fell like gentle rain upon my face, my eyes and my mouth. When my lips parted under his with a sigh, the rain became a heated storm of passion. Fear faded away. Time faded away. And the dream only tattered shreds of memory. . . .

A long while later, I gazed up at him and smiled.

"What does *dushenka* mean?"

"In English, it is difficult to express. A similar name of endearment is darling . . . but *dushenka* is much more. . . ." He paused, then kissed me. "*Dusha* is the word for soul. To a Russian, the *dusha* is very important. It expresses emotions that are most deep and close to one's heart." Taking my hand, he placed it on his chest. "You are my soul's darling, *Kasenya!* My heart's delight. . . ."

"*Dushenka* . . . ." I breathed the name in wonder. "And you are mine."

Chapter 10

CLEARING SKIES AND blackbirds singing in the fields
provided a comfortable distance from my terrifying chase the night
before. So did Charlotte's kitchen. Curled up on the window seat,
with Sergei's arms wrapped around me and the kettle on for tea, I
felt as if we were discussing what had happened to someone else.

"I am not familiar with the procedures of your police," he told
me, "but it seems unlikely they would break in and wait inside
houses."

"They don't. At least, not without a search warrant."

"Then I think we must assume those men were not Americans.
They came expecting to find Kolya and myself, and when no one
was there, they waited for your return."

I turned out of his arms to face him. "But how did they know?
Dr. Harrison had no idea you were there. I'm sure of that. And
even if Mrs. Davis suspected something, she would have called our
police. The only other person was Jeff Lloyd."

Sergei took my hand. "Try to forget for a moment that you are
American, *Kasenya*, with your lack of suspicions and your open-
ness that I so enjoy. Imagine you are Soviet, trusting no one. We
know this Jeff Lloyd had questions for Mrs. Davis. She is eager to
impress him and easily flattered. From her, he could learn much
about your 'surprise visitors.' Perhaps even a description of our
appearance. And so his suspicions grow. You, *Kasenya*, become
more interesting to him. Someone to watch. A telephone call is
made. Orders are given. They do not know, of course, but they will

watch patiently, hoping to learn more."

"But what else could they learn—even after breaking into the house? There was no evidence, nothing to show you'd been there, except the life jacket, and that could belong to anyone."

Sergei's mouth softened as he looked at me. "You are forgetting one thing, *dushenka*—my portrait in your room."

I stared blankly, then my hands went to my face. The portrait. Propped on my bed in full view for anyone to see. What better proof that Sergei and Nikolai were at the cottage. And I had given it to them.

"*Seriozha,* I'm sorry. . . ."

"Much was happening," he said, putting an arm around my shoulders. "It is understandable."

I lifted my head to look at him. "When did you see the sketch? I didn't think you noticed when we went upstairs."

"Earlier, when I went up to shower, your door was open." Sergei cupped my face in his hands. "The likeness was excellent, *dushenka*. Although I doubt KGB would appreciate your abilities as I do. . . ."

Several kisses later, we became aware of labored footsteps moving down the stairs and heard the professor's heavy cough. By the time he entered the kitchen, Sergei and I were a respectable distance apart.

Nikolai greeted me with a surprised smile. "Good morning, my dear. It is kind of you to spare me the necessity of sampling *Seriozha's* cooking, but I fear we are taking advantage of your generosity." He came forward and kissed me on each cheek. "Such a long drive so early in the morning."

"*Kasenya* arrived late last night," Sergei informed him as Nikolai took a seat at the table. The grave note in his voice quickly removed the professor's smile.

"What has happened?" he asked, looking at the two of us.

Dr. Petrovsky listened to Sergei's terse explanation, his big shoulders hunched over, his bearded face seeming much older in the pale light.

"All this is my fault," he said.

I left the window seat to put a hand on his shoulder. "Please don't blame yourself. Yesterday, when I was talking with Jeff Lloyd and Mrs. Davis, I should have been more careful."

Nikolai shook his head. "No, *Kasenya,* you do not understand. I had hoped to spare you both from danger. Instead, my silence and deception have brought it upon you."

Sergei took a chair beside his friend. "I know of no deception. Make yourself plain, Kolya. What is this you have brought upon us?"

Nikolai hesitated, then turned his eyes on me. "That first night, *Kasenya,* you asked why I was to be arrested. I answered then that one does not always know why, that KGB can make arrest for whatever reason it chooses." He sighed heavily. "This is true statement, but not for me. I know very well the reason for my arrest. A few weeks ago, I took some information from the Consulate in San Francisco." His hazel eyes met Sergei's in a plea for understanding. "It was never my intention to steal . . . only to take back what was mine . . . but what does it matter? My intentions have little value or meaning now."

"I am your friend, Kolya—not a judge of your actions or intentions. Tell me what you will."

In that moment, the depth of their friendship became evident to me, along with Sergei's unconditional loyalty. Gratitude shone in the older man's eyes, and before he glanced down, I saw his bearded chin trembling with emotion.

"Would either of you like some tea?" I said quietly. "I could make some while we talk."

"*Pazaleste* . . . please." Sergei placed my hand to his lips in an unconscious gesture before I went to the stove.

Both the kiss and the look which passed between us did not escape the professor's notice, but he made no comment.

"What kind of information was taken?" Sergei went on to ask him.

"A computer disk belonging to Grigor Markevich."

Sergei's eyes widened with shock. "Markevich! Kolya, how can this be?"

"I thought I was simply taking back the disk containing my scientific research. I never meant it to happen—a moment's impulse—" He broke off suddenly, then brushed aside his previous words with a firm, "No. That is not entirely true. Perhaps it was meant to happen all along . . . and that impulse fueled by many years of frustration."

As I brought our cups to the table on a tray, Nikolai gave me a sympathetic glance. "Probably, there is little sense in this for you, *Kasenya*. Am I correct?"

I admitted to this with a nod and asked him, "Who's Grigor Markevich?"

"A diplomatic officer at the Soviet Consulate. Only I strongly suspect that Markevich's responsibilities include more than diplomatic duties."

I felt a little ridiculous even saying the words. "You mean he's a spy?"

"He is KGB," Kolya answered soberly, then waited politely while I poured the steaming liquid before going on. "A necessary part of our stay in this country is a visit to Soviet Consulate," he explained. "One is made to feel this is only a formality—standard procedure—but this is not always so. Five years ago, on my first time here, I received a warm welcome from Consulate officials, plus much praise for my work. Immediately, I wonder what they want from me, but this I do not learn until it comes time for me to leave. Then, once more I am called into Consulate for a brief interview. The questions asked seemed valid and not unusual. What Americans had I met? What were their feelings toward the Soviet Union? Did I find the technology adequate, overwhelming, helpful? And so on.

"I knew very well the official asking these questions was a KGB colonel, in addition to his diplomatic duties. I never trusted him, but we were cordial."

"On my second visit, two years ago, I was taken to the office of Grigor Markevich. We were boyhood acquaintances in Leningrad, and I sense immediately that he wishes to use this tie for the purpose of winning my trust and confidence. Grigor and I attended the same schools and went through the ranks of Komsomol together, but we were never close. I remember how, even as a boy, Gigor understood well how to—*pokazat tovar litsom*—" He paused, searching for the English words. "Always, he could show himself at his best."

I passed Sergei the sugar for his tea. "I've heard the name before, what what exactly is Komsomol?"

"The Young Communist League" Sergei filled in. "It is organization for young people age fifteen years and older, to train and educate them in Communist ideology and the works of Lenin."

The professor gave my surprised expression a gentle smile. "You are wondering if I am devoted Party member. Let me say this. It is not always necessary to believe, but if one is to receive the privilege afforded by the Party, it is very advantageous to belong. For Grigor Markevich, the Party was his path to power.

"During our interview, Grigor had small favor to ask in return for the great privilege the Party was affording by allowing me to continue my research. The favor was information. A detailed account of University personnel, current research projects, technology, and so on. I try to rationalize by telling myself that I am doing my American colleagues no harm. Their work as marine biologists is not classified, and they are so open and eager to share, what does it matter?" He sipped the hot tea gratefully before continuing. "And so I turn in my reports, giving names of various scientists and the technology involved in their research. But inside, I am wondering what will be done with those names. Will the information I have given my country be used to follow whales for the good of science, or will that technology be used to track submarines? Is Grigor Markevich interested in my colleagues as scientists, or is he compiling a list of potential victims?

"Other questions begin to gnaw at my conscience and my sensibilities. Why should a nation as large and powerful as Soviet Union steal technology from others, yet withhold it from her own people? How can we make such great talk about *perestroika* and *glasnost* and still send a man to prison because he thinks differently than someone else? I try to suppress any feelings of disloyalty, but they continue to grow inside.

"And so, a few weeks ago, when Grigor and I are having our little chat, he asks for the disk containing my latest findings and research. I give it to him, telling myself this is the last time, when I know very well with Markevich there is never a last time. As I look at his flat face and lifeless eyes, a thought comes to me. This is what you will become—a man whose blood is warmed only by the scent of another man's blood. A man who exists without feeling!

"And then a voice tells me: No! Nikolai Matveyevich, you are worse than he. You claim to care, yet you let yourself be manipulated and used for the price of a visa.

"It was then Markevich was called out of the office. He was absent no more than a minute or two, but that was time enough for me to reach into his valise and take back what I thought was my computer disk." He took another sip of tea, then sighed.

"When did you discover you'd taken the wrong disk?" I asked.

"Not until after I had returned to University, several days later."

Sergei leaned forward. His face was grave. "Kolya . . . do you know what is on the disk?"

The professor nodded. "Names. Dates. Meetings with various individuals. Information concerning possible recruits from the American scientific community. I cannot speculate concerning its value, but if one is to judge by measures taken to get it back. . . ."

There was no need for him to continue.

"Where is the disk?" Sergei asked. "Do you have it here?"

"No. It is well hidden."

Sergei fixed the older man with a steady look.

"What good can it accomplish for you to know this?" Nikolai said. "Already, I may have told you too much."

Sergei's mouth curved in a bitter smile. "Aren't you forgetting that I am accused of Yelena's murder? What more have I to lose? At present, my situation is no better than yours." He paused. "Perhaps the computer disk could change that for both of us."

"In what way could it change things?"

"I am thinking this disk might be offered to American government in exchange for our political asylum. When your friend Miklos returns, we would not be coming to him empty-handed, begging for crumbs. Is this not so, Kasenya?"

I nodded, not knowing for sure, yet feeling a sudden glimmer of hope in the grayness that had engulfed our conversation.

Nikolai frowned and rubbed his grizzled beard. "Even if this were so, the disk cannot help us now. There is no way to get it."

"And why is this?" A wry smile played across Sergei's lips. "Surely you did not choose the bottom of the sea."

"No, but one almost as inaccessible—Bill Harrison's office in the Oceanography Building." Nikolai raised both hands in a hopeless shrug. "Neither of us can be seen near the University without being arrested or abducted . . . either one is not a pleasant choice."

I set my cup down and looked at the two men. "Maybe you can't, but I could."

Sergei stared at me. "You! Do not consider even for one moment that I will permit you to take such a risk!"

"The risks aren't that great for me. As far as the police are concerned, I don't know anything about you and Nikolai."

"*Your* police perhaps, but KGB is very much aware of your involvement. They have your description. They know your car. By this time, they may know even smallest details of your family and friends."

"If the KGB has gone to that much trouble, then they must be very disappointed. I'm from a middle-class family. My parents are happily married. My father teaches literature at a local high school and has no connections with the military. We have no secret vices, no bad debts. Think about it. In their minds, what possible motivation would I have for going after a top secret computer disk?"

Sergei sighed and shook his head. "Ah, *dushenka*. . . . I myself do not have an answer for that question."

I smiled softly and put a hand to his cheek. "Yes, you do."

Sergei pressed a kiss into my palm, then swiftly kissed my mouth with fierce possessiveness.

A purposeful cough from Nikolai drew us apart.

"I begin to see there are certain aspects of last night which you neglected to tell me." He shook his head, giving us a look that was both fond and sad.

"It is madness for *Kasenya* to consider this," Sergei said, drawing me close to his side. "Do you not agree, Kolya?"

"Madness, yes," he said quietly.

"But we can't just sit and do nothing," I argued. "If the KGB finds the disk, you'll have nothing but suspicions to offer for your freedom."

Sergei considered this with a frown, then turned to Nikolai. "Could they find it? Where in Harrison's office have you hidden the disk?"

The professor was silent, running worried fingers through his beard. "There is always the possibility that a thorough search. . . ." He drew a long breath, then looked at Sergei. "You remember Bill Harrison's portable CD player which I so admired?"

Sergei stared at him. "You hid the disk in the CD player?"

"Not in the player itself, but in one of the CDs Bill gave to me. When I discovered my mistake, I was working on the computer in Harrison's office. The enormity of what I had done was overwhelming. Bill was across the hall in the lab. I had to act quickly, and sometimes, the ridiculous can seem the most sensible. Why not hide the disk in a disk, I ask myself."

"You put a floppy disk inside a CD?" I said, thinking it would be easily discovered the moment the plastic case was opened.

"*Da*, but first I remove a black plastic container. Between this and the paper covering, there is ample space for the disk. Even if someone were to open the CD, he would not detect it. The plastic covering must be pried out," he said, gesturing with his hands. "And it is not easily removed."

Sergei gave his friend a relieved smile. "*Xeraso* . . . very good. I think we may assume that KGB will not immediately search Bill Harrison's belongings."

"At least not until after they've searched yours," I put in. "Which they've probably done by now. And if that's the case, they know the disk isn't in your apartment. It's more likely the KGB will assume Nikolai has the disk with him. If he were going to defect, or give it to the FBI, that would be the logical thing to do." I turned to Nikolai. "Which CD did you put it in? I assume Dr. Harrison has more than one in his office."

"He has several. The disk is in Tchaikovsky's '1812 Overature.'"

Sergei gave me an incredulous look. "*Dushenka*, you are not still considering —"

"We've got to try! Besides, it doesn't sound all that complicated, assuming of course, there's a way to get into Bill Harrison's office."

"Sergei and I were each given keys," Nikolai told me. "The same key allows entrance to the building as well as the labs and offices."

I smiled at the professor, then turned to Sergei. His expression was unyielding.

"Getting into Harrison's office may not be a problem," he conceded, "but to do so undetected . . . unseen? How do you propose to accomplish this?"

"I could go after hours, when no one's around."

Sergei raised his eyes. "And what makes you think you will be able to get near University before KGB discovers your presence? As I said before, they have seen your car. They have license number and description. They will be watching for you."

"All right, then. I'll take a different car. Mark's BMW is in the garage, and there's an extra set of keys upstairs in the bedroom somewhere." I looked into his dark eyes and said quietly, "I'm aware of the risks. I know it's dangerous, and I'm frightened. But I have to take the chance if you're to have any chance at all. Even without the murder charges, you've made it very clear what could happen if you're turned over to the Soviets. I have to do this, *Seriozha*. . . ."

Sergei released his frustration in some choice Russian expletives that needed no translation. "You talk to her," he said, waving a hand at Nikolai. "Maybe you can convince her what madness this is!"

Nikolai gave me that quiet, probing look of his, then slowly shook his head. "How strange to find in a young American woman those very qualities that are most beautiful and valuable in Russian women—a deeply passionate nature, tenderness, and a willingness to sacrifice herself. You could not have known this, Kasenya, but for Russian women there is a special sweetness in the willingness to sacrifice oneself. It is as strong in them as love."

Sergei put his face in his hands, and no one spoke for a long moment.

Finally, he raised his head. "You are determined to do this?"

"Yes."

He gave a slight nod. "Then, if this is how it must be, we will go together."

Chapter 11

I DON'T KNOW whether it was a sense of fatalistic calm or just a basic refusal on my part to accept the reality of what we were attempting to do, but as we discussed the details of our trip to Corvallis, I felt totally unafraid.

After a light breakfast, Nikolai had tactfully retired to the living room with a stack of *Readers' Digests* under his arm, leaving Sergei and me to wash the dishes and plan the day. Standing side by side, shoulders touching, hands in hot, soapy water, I found myself taking delight in a chore I usually avoided. Perhaps because in everything we did, no matter how simple or ordinary, there was painful poignance in knowing that the first time could also be the last.

Sergei suggested we leave after supper and plan our arrival near sunset, around nine o'clock. By that time the Oceanography Building should be empty of faculty members and students. With any luck we would also miss the custodial crew. During summer quarter there were fewer students on campus, and on a Friday night, any activities going on would be social, rather than academic.

"Do you think the police will be watching the building?" I asked.

He shook his head. "I suspect our apartment will be watched, but that is off-campus, several blocks away."

"There's still the risk that you might be recognized—especially if you wear those clothes."

Sergei glanced down at his sweatshirt with a nod.

"Mark might have something you could wear. And since I'll be staying over the weekend, I'll have to borrow some of Charlotte's things."

Sergei leaned against the counter, dish towel in hand. "I have been thinking about that. Your staying here poses certain problems."

"What kind of problems?" I tried to keep my voice casual, but Sergei was already smiling at me.

"Before you misunderstand, let me explain. I was thinking of Mrs. Davis and her dinner invitation. What will happen when she discovers you are gone? If she becomes alarmed over your absence. . . ."

"You're right. If Mrs. Davis thinks something's wrong, she might call my mother or —" I broke off with a moan. "Oh, no . . . Mrs. Davis isn't the only problem. I still haven't called Kevin!"

Sergei's dark brows lifted. "You had best call him then."

"I can't. The phone number of his hotel is back at the cottage."

"Do you know the name of this hotel?"

I shook my head, frustration growing inside me. "I was in a rush and didn't bother writing down the name. Knowing Kevin, he's probably frantic by now. I just hope he hasn't called my family and got them scared to death that something's happened to me."

Sergei took my wet hands in his and said calmly, "Then we must find a reasonable way of calming their fears. Tell me, *dushenka,* if I had not so rudely intruded upon your life, what sort of pleasant activity would occupy your weekend?"

I smiled and wrapped my arms around his neck. "Have I mentioned how glad I am that you 'so rudely intruded upon my life?'"

"Not in words perhaps. . . ." he began, kissing the corners of my mouth.

Some time later, he smiled at me and said, "I find this activity most pleasant, *Kasenya,* but we must think of another to satisfy your family."

"Mmmm, I guess you're right." I sighed and thought a moment. "If you weren't here, then it might be fun to pack my paints and travel up the coast."

"An excellent plan," he agreed. "Knowing your impulsive nature, Kevin would not be surprised to learn of this. Nor would Mrs. Davis."

"But how am I supposed to let Kevin know without a phone number?"

"Perhaps your family could relay the message. In any case, it would be good for them to know you will be away."

"I'll call Mom and Mrs. Davis right now." I paused, hand on the receiver. "What if Mrs. Davis has found out who you are?"

"If she knows, she knows," he said, nonplussed by the possibility. "And it would be far better for us to know as well. If that is the case, say nothing and hang up the phone. But if she is still believing I am your fiance, then we can take advantage of this for a short while longer."

A short while longer. As I dialed Mrs. Davis' number, I couldn't help wondering how brief that time might be, then shoved the question aside. *Seriozha* was with me now. I couldn't bear thinking beyond that.

Mrs. Davis readily accepted my explanation and proposed plans for the weekend. My fears that she might have discovered Sergei and Nikolai's real identities vanished as she repeatedly expressed her disappointment over the postponed dinner invitation.

"Such a handsome young man," she told me. "And so polite. You be sure to let me know the next time he comes, and I'll cook a salmon dinner he'll never forget!"

My mother was delighted to hear from me and full of typical motherly precautions and instructions. Another time I would have reminded her that I was twenty-five years old and had lived on my own for the past three years. But now, listening to the love and concern in her voice, I felt a sudden wave of sadness. If something went wrong in Corvallis. . . . I tried to push away the possibility, but it refused to leave. If something went wrong . . . this might be the last time we talked together.

There was a lump in my throat as I asked her relay the message to Kevin if he happened to call. "I've lost the number of his hotel," I lied, "and I don't want him to worry. . . ."

"I'll be sure to tell him, honey. Now you be careful and have a nice time."

"I will Mom . . . and thanks. I love you."

I hung up before the tears started to flow, and Sergei took me in his arms. He didn't say anything, just held me and let me cry.

I stepped back, wiped my eyes with his dish towel, and drew a long breath. "Let's go upstairs and find you some clothes."

Sergei stood staring at the racks of suits, shirts, sweaters, and slacks on Mark's half of the huge walk-in closet.

"All this belongs only to your brother-in-law?" he said with more bewilderment than envy.

I nodded, smiling, as he fingered the soft sleeve of a brown leather jacket.

"*Basnoslovnyi, . . .*" he murmured. "Arkasha would be content to stand in line for a month to wear something as fine as this."

"Arkasha?"

"My brother."

"Would you like to try it on?"

"No need. It is too impractical."

You're right, I thought. Four hundred dollars worth of impractical.

I sorted through some casual shirts and sweaters, then took a hooded jacket off its hanger. "Here's something that might be useful. I doubt it'll be cold in Corvallis, but the hood should keep people from getting a good look at you."

"Very good, *dushenka*," he said, holding the jacket up for fit. "This will do well."

"And how about this?" I slipped a v-necked cotton sweater off its hanger, thinking how well the deep teal color would suit his dark good looks.

Sergei pulled his sweatshirt over his head, and I felt an unsettling physical response to the sight of him.

I held his sweatshirt while he tried on the sweater, his broad shoulders stretching the soft fabric in a way Mark's slighter build never would.

"How do you say 'very handsome' in Russian?"

His smile sent my pulse rate soaring.

Dropping his sweatshirt on a shelf, I turned to Charlotte's side of the closet, my hands mechanically sorting through the clothes, while I tried to get my emotions under control.

Sergei moved behind me, wrapped both arms around my middle and proceeded to plant a warm kiss on my neck.

I leaned against him with a shaky sigh. "How am I supposed to find something if you keep distracting me . . . ?"

He laughed softly. "Then I will make the choice."

I watched as Sergei deftly sorted through my sister's wardrobe, frowning at some of her favorite clothes, raising an eyebrow at others.

"Ah . . . here is something."

I smiled at the scanty, peach-colored concoction he held out to me and shook my head. "Too impractical."

Sergei's dark eyes were warm with desire. "What a shame, *dushenka*, that we must be so practical. . . ."

Nikolai came into the kitchen as I was preparing lunch and found me gazing wistfully out the window.

"No matter how attractive the bars, the cage bird still longs to fly free . . . is it not so, Cassandra?"

I shook away my moment's longing to give him a cheerful smile. "I was just thinking what a beautiful day it is. What would you like for lunch, Kolya—cold cuts and cheese or leftover spaghetti?"

"Prepare whatever pleases you. I am not hungry." He covered his mouth to cough, and the harsh, heavy sound filled me with concern.

"Have you taken any medicine this morning?"

He nodded, trying to clear his throat, and I brought him a glass of water.

"Thank you, my dear. I am feeling much better." Nikolai

smiled at my worried frown and said, "I will not have you worrying about an old man on a day so beautiful as this." He looked out the kitchen window where mild sunshine warmed fields sprinkled with daisies and blue cornflowers. His eyes were tender and far away. "I remember a day such as this with my Anna. All of life seemed a miracle because we could share it together." He sighed and turned to me. "Anna brought food for us in a small basket, covered with a fine linen napkin. We dined on hard-cooked eggs, *kolbasa* and brown bread and thought we had a meal any king would envy. Strange, how even the smallest details return so clearly. When I see you and *Seriozha* smile together when you think I am not noticing . . . ah, how the memories come rushing back." Nikolai turned his gaze to the window once more. "I have noticed the woods on the hill above us . . . so secluded. An ideal spot to take a picnic lunch. Do you not agree, *Kasenya?*"

I put my hands on his big shoulders and kissed his bearded cheek. "I'll start boiling the eggs."

Sergei and I sat on an old quilt, under a canopy of fragrant fir. The air was soft, with drowsy warmth. Above us, slanted sunlight and blue sky filtered through lacy green boughs. From somewhere below, a cow's gentle lowing colored the silence.

Sergei stretched out on the quilt, with his dark head in my lap. I looked down at him, running my fingers through the thickness of his hair.

The tenuous future . . . what might or might not be . . . was not mentioned. In some ways I didn't want to know what lay ahead for us. Sergei seemed to understand this without my saying a word.

Looking up at me, he asked, "Tell me something about your family . . . your parents . . . about yourself, as a child."

I smiled. "My father's name is Robert. I grew up listening to him quote Shakespeare and Wordsworth and Walt Whitman. My mother's name is Rosemary, and she's just like her name—sweet, old-fashioned, loving. Mom adores flowers, and they adore her. She can make anything bloom. My sisters are a lot like her. Charlotte always did everything right, and Emily was so sweet it didn't matter whether she was right or not."

Sergei's hand on my wrist was softly caressing. "And you?"

I smiled self-consciously. "I was . . . different . . . part tomboy, part romantic. One minute begging to go fishing with the neighbor boys, and the next, a fairy tale princess or a mermaid —"

"Or a *rusalka?*" he filled in.

I smiled down at him, remembering his description of the wood nymph who haunted forest pools. "Grandpa Hugh understood me better than anyone else. I was born on his birthday, so my parents let him choose my name. When I was home, I managed to be sensible and obedient for Mom's sake, but whenever I was at the cottage, my imagination ran wild. I could be anything there . . . dream anything. And Grandpa Hugh encouraged me to paint those dreams."

"I wish I could have known him."

"In some ways, Nikolai reminds me a lot of Grandpa Hugh. I know he would have loved you both," I added quietly, stroking the softness of his hair. "Poor Mom. She wasn't so sure her father was a very good influence on me. She used to get so frustrated, trying to convince me that real life couldn't be the way it was in fairy tales."

"And did you believe her?"

"I tried, but it didn't stop me from dreaming. Kevin's always telling me I need to be more practical, too, but —" I stopped and glanced away, never intending to mention his name.

Sergei drew my hand to his lips and kissed my fingertips. "I enjoy it very much when you are not practical."

I leaned down to meet his kiss, then he whispered, "Come, lie beside me."

We lay in each other's arms, looking up at the blue between the boughs.

"What's Natalya like?"

Sergei was silent for a moment, then he said, "Tasha is a very good person."

The dark-haired beauty by Botticelli that I had created in my mind suddenly took on human form and ceased to be a threat. It might be wicked, but I knew I would much rather be a *rusalka* than a *very good person.*

"We met at University," he continued. "Tasha was also studying to be a marine biologist. She is very bright. Very ambitious."

"Oh."

There was another long silence. Then he asked, "Did you meet Kevin while you were attending art school?"

"No. I was invited to a friend's party in Portland last year, and he was there."

"Mmmm."

We turned at the same moment and looked into each other's eyes.

"Oh, *Seriozha* . . . What are we going to do?"

His answer was not in words, but his kiss left no doubts as to his meaning.

Chapter 12

WE DROVE AWAY in the green-gold light of late afternoon.

Nikolai's last words to us lingered long in my mind, as did the sight of his stocky figure standing beside the garage, still dignified, even in wrinkled, disheveled clothes. After kissing us on both cheeks, in turn, he looked into our faces for a long moment. "God keep you safe," he had said.

"You are thoughtful," Sergei commented as we passed through a small farming community a few miles south of Tillamook. "If you have second thoughts about our venture, I will understand."

"It's not that. I was thinking about Nikolai. He told me he was a communist, and yet he believes in God."

Sergei nodded. "In Soviet Union, we have a phrase for this. Some would call Kolya a 'raddish Russian'—red on the outside, white on the inside. There are many who pay lip-service to Party ideology. Belief or nonbelief is not the issue, so long as one submits to the system and does not challenge it openly. One must learn how to 'double-think.' It can be very difficult at times, to carry the truth inside—to find some measure of private honesty—and yet, live a public lie."

I stared at him. "I can't imagine living like that."

"I don't believe you could, *dushenka*. Not after experiencing freedom. But when one knows no different. . . ."

My sideways glance was openly curious. "Are you . . . a 'raddish Russian?'"

"Until three days ago," he said quietly. "There comes a time when one is forced to—*shrasyvat masku*—to throw off the mask, in a matter of speaking. When I learned of Kolya's arrest, I had to choose." He was silent for a long while, from all outward appearances absorbed in the passing landscape. Then he turned to me. "I wish you to know, *dushenka,* that while I am *partiiny*—a party member—my *dusha* is not. My father was Russian and an atheist. My mother is Christian. Her family is of Latvian and Polish descent."

My eyes widened. "That's quite an unlikely combination."

"The divison in their backgrounds and beliefs was not as great as it would appear. Father was a kind man who hated injustice of any kind. He was a frustrated idealist who saw only the ideals of communism—not the reality of how it was practiced.

"And so at school, I hear the glories of Lenin, and I am taught that all religion is decadent and dangerous to the state. At home, I hear my mother's prayers and verses from a Bible telling me to love my brother and love God. There were times when it was very confusing, very difficult for me. But gradually, I began to see the difference in what was said and what was done." His mouth curved in a bitter smile. "In Soviet Union, we have free medical care, *dushenka,* but my best friend died because he was diabetic and could not get insulin. My mother has had to stand in line for hours to buy a bar of soap, while the privileged buy whatever they want on black market. Inside, I tell myself, if these are examples of the glories and goodness of Lenin, then I want no part of it. From that time, truth becomes a passion with me. I pour my efforts into my studies and research. There, I did not have to make lies for appearance sake. Or so I thought, until I was asked to make reports on Kolya."

"You've more than made up for that now," I said.

Sergei stared out the window. "I hope so. . . ."

We had been on the road perhaps half an hour when we left Highway '101' for a winding forest road known as 'Sourgrass' which followed the Nestucca River.

Slanting gold light filtered through the deep green of Douglas firs, the lighter, lacier green of hemlocks and luxuriant ferns. Moss grew everywhere, on trunks, limbs and vines, while purple foxglove, red elderberries and the pink of wild roses added color to the roadside.

The BMW handled the road's twisting curves with flawless ease, but I found myself suffering from the effects of last night's harrowing chase. That, plus the fact I was driving my brother-in-law's most prized possession, made it difficult to relax and enjoy the scenery.

In the midst of a twisting series of curves, a gray Toyota cruised up on our tail and doggedly refused to back off. The driver probably had no ulterior motives in mind, other than impatience to get by, but that was all it took for blinding headlights to flash in my memory. My hands instantly tightened on the wheel, and I pressed down on the gas, trying to increase the distance between us.

Sergei's hand on my shoulder and quiet voice broke through my fierce concentration. "Pull over, *Kasenya*. . . . Allow him to pass."

I switched on the blinker, slowed and pulled onto the shoulder at the first opportunity.

Without a word, he slid over beside me, gently massaging my neck and shoulders. His sure, knowing hands found the tight knots of tension and eased them away.

I released a long sigh. "I'm sorry. Having that Toyota come up behind us like that suddenly reminded me of last night, and I guess I panicked."

"It is understandable."

"Plus, I can't help worrying about the stupid car."

Sergei frowned. "Is something wrong with its functioning? I had not noticed."

"The car's fine. But if I get so much as a scratch on it, Mark'll kill me."

"And this is the cause of your worry?"

I gave him a sheepish look. "Mark's only had the car for a few months."

He laughed and shook his head. "You must tell me about this brother-in-law who inspires more fear in you than KGB."

I laughed, too, and the last of my tension melted away.

We drove into Corvallis as the glow of sunset was fading into dusk. Sergei directed me to the northwest corner of campus where the Oceanography building was located. Looking at the large red brick building, I felt a nervous flutter in the pit of my stomach.

"The labs are all located in the front part of the building," Sergei told me as we drove slowly past. "In the back are the offices."

A large parking area behind the building was empty, well lighted, and for our purposes, far too conspicuous. I found a space on the adjacent street and switched off the engine. The back of the building was nearly all windows. The first and third floors were totally dark; three lights burned on the second.

"Harrison's office is on the second floor," Sergei pointed out. "The fourth window from the end." He sucked in his breath. "Harrison is there . . . talking with someone."

I followed Sergei's gaze to one of the lighted windows. Bill Harrison stood near a blackboard, his bearded face easily recognizable. The visitor was sitting with his back to the window, and I could see little more than the top of his blond head.

"What do we do now?"

Sergei leaned back against the seat, pulling the hood of his jacket up to conceal his face. "We wait."

The street was quiet. In five minutes, only two cars passed by. I turned my attention back to the office window on the second floor. "Dr. Harrison seems upset. Whoever it is he's talking to, he must not like what he's saying."

A moment later, the visitor got to his feet and turned casually toward the window.

I gasped and gripped Sergei's arm. "The man with Harrison! That's Jeff Lloyd."

"You are sure of this?" When I nodded, Sergei frowned and stared thoughtfully at the man framed in the lighted window. "I wonder what it is he hopes to learn. . . ."

As we watched, Dr. Harrison moved to the door and Lloyd followed. The office blinked into blackness.

"We will wait a few minutes more," Sergei told me. "To make

certain both men have gone."

I glanced back at the second floor where two lights still burned in other rooms. "As long as there's someone else in the building, I don't think you should risk going in." Answering Sergei's sharp look, I went on quickly, "I can be in and out in no time. All you have to do is give me some instructions and the key. If I do run into someone, I'll just act like I know what I'm doing."

I took his silence as an encouraging sign. "Look, I know you're familiar with the building, but this is too important for you to risk being seen. All it would take is for someone to walk out of one of those offices while you're there."

Sergei rubbed the flat of his hand along his thigh, then glanced up the street where Dr. Harrison had just exited from the west end of the building. Walking beside him was Jeff Lloyd. The two men crossed the street where a tan Subaru was parked against the curb. After giving the journalist a curt nod, Harrison got in his car and drove away. Lloyd watched the departing car for a few seconds, then crossed the street and headed down the sidewalk in our direction.

I turned to Sergei in a cold panic. "What are we going to do? He'll be sure to see us!"

"Then what he sees must convince him that his presence means nothing to us," Sergei answered and took me in his arms.

A few minutes later, I released a shaky sigh and said, "I don't know about Jeff Lloyd, but I'm convinced."

Sergei glanced cautiously over his shoulder, then kissed me again. "Lloyd is gone."

"Good. How about the key and some directions?"

He hesitated, and I said softly. "I'll be fine, *dushenka.* You know it's the safest way."

Sergei took a silver key from his jeans pocket and put it into my hand. "This will open outside doors as well as office and labs. The stairway to the second floor is near the west entrance where Harrison left. His office is 240-E."

I nodded. "Where do you suggest I look for the CD?"

"The player itself is usually on the desk. The CD . . ." His shoulders lifted in an expressive shrug. "It could be anywhere.

Harrison's methods of organization are best understood only by himself."

I smiled and leaned over to kiss him. "See you in a few minutes."

A car approached as I unlocked the heavy outside door, and I felt naked in the passing glare of its headlights. Then I was inside the building and running up the stairs.

The long hallway on the second floor was dark, empty and silent. Near the opposite end, I could see pale light shining from the small windows of two office doors. Clutching the key in my hand, I walked swiftly down the hall, my rubber-soled sneakers noiseless on the smoothly-polished floors. A few more seconds to find office 240-E, a simple turn of the key, and I was inside.

I felt around the wall for the light switch and had a moment's panic as the overhead light exposed my presence to the outside. I hurried to the window. I wasn't able to reach the top of the blind without standing on a chair, and its simple scrape seemed louder than a lion's roar.

The shade drawn, I turned my attention to the office contents. Notebooks, folders, loose paper, and several thick textbooks were strewn across the desk top. To my right, a bookcase filled nearly half the wall. A metal filing cabinet was squeezed into a corner with rolled up charts, more folders and some periodicals stacked on top.

I searched the desk first, trying not to disturb the contents, but failed to find the CD player, let alone any CDs. Two of the desk drawers were locked, and a third contained only manilla file folders and office supplies. I painstakingly went through the shelves of the bookcase and the top of the filing cabinet with the same results. My searching glance spotted something dark and squarish on the windowsill, stuffed between two appointment books. My heart skipped a beat, then sank as I picked up a recording of Beethoven's 6th Symphony. I tossed it aside.

As I glanced around the small office, wondering where to look next, a discomforting thought came to mind. What if the CD player and the disk were not in the office at all? What if Dr. Harrison had taken them home for the weekend?

I rummaged through the desk once more, this time not caring if the contents were disturbed, then turned out the light and shut the door behind me.

One look at my face gave Sergei the results of my search.

"Do you think Dr. Harrison might have taken it home with him?"

Sergei shook his head, rejecting the possibility. "There is no need. At his home, Harrison has a much larger sound system. It is possible the CD player and the disk could have been moved to Kolya's office or one of the labs."

"Which lab is his?"

Sergei took my hand. "No, *dushenka*. This time we go together."

A bewildering display of scientific equipment met my gaze as Sergei ushered me into Bill Harrison's lab and shut the door. The room was long and narrow, with floor to ceiling metal shelves extending halfway into the room on our left, lab tables and equipment on the right, and a narrow aisle between.

I glanced at Sergei. "Where do we start?"

He smiled at my expression. "I will take the back, you the front, and we will meet in the middle."

The CD player was sitting in plain sight on one of the lab tables. A heavy plastic cover from a microscope had been carelessly tossed over the top, or I would have noticed it sooner. Half-covered by a metal clipboard and two notebooks were three CDs. The second one I picked up contained Tchaikovsky's 1812 Overature.

My heartbeat quickened as I opened the plastic case, removed the bright silver disk and set it aside. With my thumb and finger-nails, I carefully pried off the black plastic container. Resting between it and the paper sleeve was a floppy disk. Flat. Black. Innocuous.

I turned around and started to whistle the Overature's familiar theme, just as the lab door opened and Jeff Lloyd sauntered into the room.

"Well, Miss Graves," he said, flashing me a pleased, confident smile. "How nice to see you again."

Chapter 13

I STOOD SPEECHLESS, as Jeff Lloyd shut the door behind him. He glanced at the plastic case in my hands with a grudging smile.

"Very clever of Petrovsky to hide the disk inside a CD. You've just saved me a lot of searching, Miss Graves." Stepping toward me, he held out his hand.

I backed down the narrow aisle between the shelves and lab tables.

There's no point in you making this difficult," he said. "There's no where you can go."

I took another step back. "How did you know I was here?"

Lloyd smiled and put his hands in his pockets. "You're obviously an intelligent young woman or Petrovsky wouldn't have trusted you to get the disk, but I'm afraid your lack of experience in these matters is equally obvious. I was planning to come back and search Harrison's office myself when I saw you standing in front of the window. Next time, you'd be smart to lower the blind before you turn on the lights. Not that there will be a next time." His mouth hardened. "The disk, Miss Graves."

When I didn't answer, he gave a careless shrug. "Fine. If you don't want to give the disk to me, we can wait a few minutes for my friends to arrive."

"Those friends wouldn't happen to have Russian names would they?"

His blue eyes were intent on my face. "I'm impressed, Miss Graves. But I haven't quite figured out who's paying you or why you're doing this." He motioned to a stool near one of the lab tables. "Sit down. You might as well be comfortable while we wait."

I backed against the metal edge of a shelf containing glass jars with samples of algae and seawater. "Who's paying you, Mr. Lloyd?" I asked, my fingers finding and closing around one of the glass jars. "Or does it matter? Maybe you're one of those pathetic parasites who'll sell anything, including himself, to the highest bidder."

Lloyd's smile turned ugly, and he made a sudden lunge toward me. I flung the bottle at his face, but it only hit his shoulder a glancing blow before shattering on the floor. The next moment Sergei stepped from behind the tall shelf at the back of the lab.

"Take the disk and go, *Kasenya*," he ordered calmly.

Shock widened Lloyd's blue eyes, then he was diving toward the door to block my exit.

"Neither one of you is going anywhere."

"And why not?" Sergei asked, walking toward him. "There is no one here to stop us."

Lloyd stiffened and stood his ground, then made a wild swing. Sergei dodged the blow, seized the man's wrist and spun him around, twisting Lloyd's arm behind his back. Grunting and straining from the pain, Lloyd bent forward, then lashed out with a vicious kick. The move cost him his footing on the wet floor and he went down, pulling Sergei on top of him.

His head hit the glass-splintered floor with a hard crack, pain exploded across his features, then the journalist slumped and lay still.

I rushed forward as Sergei got to his feet. "Are you all right?"

He nodded, pulling a sliver of glass from his hand. "I would have taken him sooner, but I thought he had a gun. You have the disk?"

I smiled and held it out to him.

Sergei took it from me with a quick kiss, then motioned to the door. "Quickly! We must go!"

The sound of voices drifted up to us before we reached the bottom of the stairs. We froze and listened. When I heard a nasal voice inquiring about a baseball score, my pent-up breath came out in a gush. Sergei and I moved quietly down the remaining stairs, and I peered around the corner.

Two custodians stood barely ten feet away, arguing the merits of various players and debating the umpire's calls.

Sergei nodded for me to follow him up the stairs, and we sprinted back to the second floor.

"There are more stairs and another exit at the end of this hall, but we must hurry!"

We raced down the dark hall, past labs and offices, then down the flight of stairs. Sergei motioned for me to wait while he checked the exit and returned seconds later.

"Come!" He grabbed my hand, and we dashed for the door.

Outside, Sergei glanced cautiously at the shadowy, tree-lined walks, then led me around the edge of the building. Keeping to the shadows, we skirted the edge of the parking lot and paused in the rustling cover of a large maple. Barely thirty yards down the sidewalk, the BMW sat next to the curb.

Sergei scanned the street and nearby houses. "Have the keys ready," he said and stepped out of the shadows.

Those thirty yards were the longest I have ever walked. One car passed by without slowing or stopping. Across the street, a porch light came on, then a screen door opened and an elderly woman stooped over to pick up her cat. A young man whizzed past on a ten-speed. Then we were inside the car with the doors locked and the engine humming to life at the first turn of the key.

I think we must have been halfway to Monmouth before my hands stopped shaking.

We passed through quiet towns, along the straight stretch toward Rickreall, then on to Valley Junction, without incident or the least cause for suspicion.

During the entire time, Sergei spoke barely a handful of sentences. Even in the darkness I could sense the rigid alertness of his body, and when his gaze wasn't fastened on the sideview mirror, he was checking the road behind us.

"What's wrong?" I said finally. "Do you think we're being followed?"

"For the present, it would not seem so."

"Then what's bothering you?"

"It was too simple," he answered. "Too easy."

"What was too easy?"

"KGB was alerted to our presence. We know how much they desire the disk. And yet, we are allowed to drive away."

"Lloyd said his friends were coming, but we don't know from where. Maybe we got lucky and our timing was right."

"Perhaps," he said, "but it still seems to simple."

I drew a long breath. "When Jeff Lloyd showed up, I thought things were going to get very complicated."

"He must have been the one following us yesterday. This Mr. Lloyd gets around."

I nodded, stared thoughtfully at the straight stretch of road illuminated by our headlights. "An American journalist working for the KGB. I wonder what his newspaper would think about that?"

"A valuable asset for the Party, one must admit," Sergei said. "The opportunities for pro-Soviet propoganda and disinformation would be many." He gave the road behind us another glance. "How much longer before we reach Tillamook?"

"Mmm, another half-hour, forty-five minutes maybe." I glanced over at him with an encouraging smile. "We're going to make it, you know."

Sergei's voice was grave. "I pray God it will be so."

There was very little traffic by the time we reached Sourgrass. I slowed and turned the lights on high beam, giving the winding forest road my full attention.

A few minutes later, Sergei asked quietly, "Is there another way—a different route we could take to your sister's house?"

Something in his voice sent cold dread through my veins. "Are we being followed?"

He gave a short nod and put a hand on my knee.

"How long have you known?"

"Not long, but I have felt it for some time. They are keeping a large space of distance behind us."

"Are you sure?"

"Inside, I am sure. I think they intend for us to lead them to

Nikolai. Otherwise they would have pulled us over before now."

"Not necessarily. There was too much traffic before."

He conceded to this with a nod. "In either case, we cannot return the way we came."

"In a few minutes, we'll be getting to Hebo Junction."

"What are our choices there?"

"Only two. Highway 101 into Tillamook or the road to Lincoln City." I bit my lip, trying to think. "I've only been on the Lincoln City road a couple of times, but if I remember right, it's fairly straight and open. If we stay on 101, there's one other turn-off —"

"You must decide, *Kasenya.*"

I felt a moment's panicky indecision when the sign for Hebo Junction appeared. On the left, the road to Lincoln City beckoned, but something kept me on the road toward Beaver and Tillamook. Glancing in the rearview mirror, I saw headlights approach the junction, slow, then follow us on 101.

We had barely reached Beaver when a car pulled out in front of us, forcing me to slacken speed.

"Oh, great . . . that's all we need."

"How far to this other turn-off?" Sergei asked, his voice tight.

"It should be coming up in less than a mile, if I remember right." Staring at the taillights in front of us, an idea flashed through my mind. I gave Sergei a sideways glance. "Are you ready for some evasive maneuvers?"

"I am not sure of your meaning, *dushenka,* but with you, I am ready for anything."

The warm trust in his voice gave my flagging confidence a much-needed boost. I waited until we rounded a short series of curves, then sank my foot onto the gas. The distance between us and the red taillights ahead was eaten up in seconds. We came barreling up behind the car just as we reached the Sand Lake turn-off. Pulling a hard left, I gunned up the hilly road, then swung onto the shoulder, under a dark cover of trees. I switched off the lights and shifted the transmission into Park. Not fifteen seconds later, a dark car whipped around the last curve on the road below us and raced down the dark stretch of highway.

As soon as it passed by, I turned the headlights back on and accelerated up the Sand Lake road. "By the time they realize they're following the wrong car, we'll have several minutes head start."

"And where will this road take us?"

"Past the dunes, onto Cape Lookout Mountain. Once we're down the mountain we can choose from a couple of routes—Netarts or Oceanside. Even if they do doubleback, they won't know which road we've taken."

Sergei stretched an arm along the back of my seat, and I felt his warm fingers on my neck. "After our return, you must remind me to demonstrate the depth of my appreciation, *dushenka*."

His husky voice sent a pleasant shiver of anticipation through me. Smiling, I said, "Consider yourself reminded."

In minutes, we had passed by the moonlit dunes, and the road began a curving climb into dense forests. Groves of alders and towering Douglas fir pressed close on either side as the BMW purred effortlessly up the mountain. Once past the summit, the road took us down in a series of tight s-curves. Our need for speed was greater than the need for caution, and I swooped down the road, taking the curves faster than I'd ever dare in daylight. Coming out of a curve, I pressed on the gas, wanting to take full advantage of the straight stretch ahead.

Something leaped out of the blackness, red eyes caught the headlights' glare, then there was a sickening thud. I slammed on the brakes, but it was already too late. The force of impact sent the deer flying up over the hood, smashing into the windshield. Glass splintered into a thousand white veins. I hung onto the wheel and rammed my foot onto the brake pedal as the car skidded wildly. We shuddered to a stop, and the silence was deafening.

I unbuckled my seat belt, then reached for Sergei.

His hands gripped my shoulders. "Are you hurt?"

"No. I don't think so. . . . I didn't see the deer. I'm sorry. I didn't see it. . . ."

"*Kasenya,* we must go! If KGB has doubled back, they may be following not far behind."

The urgency in his voice broke through the shock, and I quickly followed him out of the car.

Moonlight fell on a large, dark shape a few yards away.

Sergei ran toward the deer, and I cringed at the sight of its twitching legs and warm body.

"It's still alive," I choked.

"*Nyet, Kasenya,*" he told me, bending down beside the animal. "The neck is broken. It is dead. Get cover for yourself, while I take it from the road."

I stumbled off onto the shoulder and stood, arms around my sides, as Sergei grabbed hold of the deer's front legs and dragged it off the asphalt into the trees.

"We must hope they do not notice the blood," he said, running back to me.

"What are we going to do with the car?" Besides the broken windshield, the right front fender was badly dented into the wheel.

Sergei glanced toward a thick cover of brush and alders on the left side of the road. "We must get it into those trees."

I quickly climbed into the driver's seat, breathing a thankful sigh as the engine hummed into life. Leaning out the window, I followed Sergei's directing arm, slowly easing the car off the road. It scraped forward, the wheel pulling badly to the left. There was barely enough room between two sturdy trunks for the BMW to squeeze through. The car limped a few more feet into the brush before another tree blocked its path. I locked the car, offering my brother-in-law a silent apology, then hurried back to the roadside where Sergei was watching the steep s-curve above us.

Without a word, he took my hand, and together we walked down the mountain road into the concealing blackness of the night.

ChapteR 14

SERGEI AND I hadn't been walking long when the smooth hum of an engine warned us of a car's approach. In seconds, we were off the shoulder and melting into the black shadows of the forest.

The dark car passed by at a moderate speed, too fast to give even a moment's glimpse of the occupants. Sergei waited until the sound of its engine had died in the distance before moving on. We kept to the trees as much as possible, choosing the comfort of the roadside only when the forest was too dense or the going too steep.

The night air was cool, but not bitter. Our jackets provided ample warmth against its moist chill. Although we couldn't see it, I knew from the unmistakable tang in the air that the ocean was somewhere below. We walked in silence, hands clasped, ears alert for the faint grumble of an engine.

"Are you frightened?" Sergei asked, squeezing my hand.

"A little. Do you think they'll come back?"

"Yes."

Minutes later, the car returned.

Crouched behind a dense cover of trees and foliage, Sergei and I watched its slow, deliberate approach. My heart felt as if it were slamming against my ribs, and I hardly dared breathe.

"They are uncertain what to do," Sergei whispered, as the dark car passed. "Return to the main highway or turn around. Either way, they will lose precious time in finding us."

"What if they see the car? They might notice something. . . ."

Sergei drew a taut breath, considering the possibility. "Being unfamiliar with the area, I doubt they would attempt to search for us on foot. If they return again soon, we will know. . . ."

The foliage was damp underfoot and around my legs. As we waited in the darkness, I could feel the cold penetrating my clothes. Only the rustle of the breeze and the cry of a night bird broke the silence. Still, Sergei waited. My muscles ached. One foot was asleep, but I said nothing.

A low hum throbbed on the night air, growing to the unmistakable sound of an approaching vehicle. Sergei's arm tightened around me as headlights appeared around the forested bend above us.

The car passed by at a good speed, never slowing. I knew in a moment that it was a different make, smaller, lighter in color. I glanced at Sergei.

"Not yet," he said softly.

Scarcely a minute later, another pair of headlights flashed around the dark curve. A chill gripped my heart as I recognized the vehicle. Sergei waited long after its taillights had disappeared into the winding blackness below before giving me a nod and helping me to my feet.

My joints were stiff, and my steps shaky, but it was good to walk again. We must have covered more than a mile before Sergei asked, "Where will this road take us?"

"Once we get down the mountain, we'll be on Whiskey Creek Road near Netarts."

"Whiskey Creek?" he repeated. "It sounds inviting, but right now I would be happy for a drink of water."

I smiled at him. "Me, too."

"How much farther to this Whiskey Creek?"

"Mmm, I'm not sure. At least three miles."

"Are you able to walk that distance?"

"I'm fine."

Above us, the pale moon cast a blue-white glow, and stars glittered. On either side, the silent forest watched our passage. Sergei held my hand and I took comfort from its warmth. Somehow, his tall figure striding beside me made the night seem less threatening.

"I'm glad you're here," I said.

Sergei looked at me, and his voice was tinged with sadness. "If I were not here, *Kasenya,* you would not be placed in this situation—but safely asleep at your Winwood Cottage."

I pressed his hand to my cheek. "I'm still glad you're here."

His reply was in Russian, and there was only one word I understood—*dushenka.*

I smiled up at him. "That makes two translations you owe me."

"What?"

"What you just said and the one yesterday—about your 'poetic fire,' was how Nikolai described it."

He laughed, then grew serious. "I owe you much more than translations, *Kasenya.*"

During the next hour, only one car passed by on the mountain road. The steep down hill grade leveled out, and the smell of the sea was much stronger.

I tried not to think how far we had come, how much farther we might have to go, but soon, it took all my concentration just to keep walking.

"Nikolai must be worried sick about us," I said. "I wish we could get to a phone and let him know we're safe."

"How can we telephone? If I am seen. . . ."

"I know, but we can't walk all the way back to Tillamook. Even if I were up to a brisk, twenty mile hike, we'd never make it before morning."

Sergei put an arm around my waist and asked, "But how can we risk asking for help or a place to stay?"

"I don't know. . ." I said and walked wearily on.

After another mile or so, an isolated farmhouse came into view. We trudged on, passing half a dozen more. Then, off to the left, I noticed what appeared to be an attractive two-story farmhouse with a shake-cedar roof. The house was set well back from the road on a wooded hillside overlooking Netarts Bay. On the curving drive below the house, a quaint lamp post illuminated a sign half hidden by vines. I stopped and grabbed Sergei's arm.

"That's a bed and breakfast inn. I think we've just found our phone and a place to stay."

Sergei frowned, and I went on quickly. "I'll talk to the owners. It'll be all right."

"And what will you tell them?"

"The truth. That we hit a deer and damaged the car."

Sergei gave a reluctant nod, and we turned our steps toward the sloping gravel drive.

The woman who answered my knock was young, no more than thirty, with long dark braids hanging down her back and a fussy infant in her arms. She listened to my apology and explanation, all the while swaying back and forth, patting the baby.

"You didn't get me up," she said with a tired smile. "Little Josh has been doing a good job of that for six months now. Where'd you hit the deer?"

"Coming down the mountain, not too far past the summit."

She nodded. "There's deer all through there. You folks've had quite a walk." She smiled, including Sergei in her sympathetic glance. "I'm Doris Hopkins. What was the name again?"

"Graves," I answered quickly, returning her smile. "Alex and Cassie Graves."

"Well, you're in luck. There's one vacancy left. The Dolphin Room. I'll be right back with the key."

I turned to Sergei, who stood in the shadows away from the revealing porch light. "The Dolphin Room . . . that sounds like ideal quarters for an oceanographer."

He smiled and pulled me close for a hard kiss.

"Here's the key," came a voice from the doorway. "That'll be $55.00."

I glanced around to see Doris Hopkins watching us with a broad smile. "Will my Visa card be all right?" I asked her, retrieving my wallet from the jacket pocket.

"That'll be fine. Are you two on your honeymoon?" she inquired, dark eyes shining.

"Well, you might say it's sort of an impromptu honeymoon."

The woman gave me a knowing look and took the card. "I'll be right back with your receipt. The Dolphin Room's up those stairs," she directed, pointing to a rustic stone stairway curving up to the second story. "First door on your right. Breakfast is served between eight and ten, but if you want to sleep in, I'll save you something."

The Dolphin Room was aptly decorated in marine colors of green and blue with panelled walls and a beamed ceiling. Hanging over the queen-sized bed was a framed poster of two dolphins leaping joyously out of the waves. The furnishings were a quaint mixture of Cape Cod and Victorian—crisp white linens, an old-fashioned pitcher and wash basin on the dresser, brass lamps and an antique barometer. On the western wall, wide windows opened up to the sea.

I stood for a moment, letting the feelings of warmth and safety wash over me, appreciating them as I never had before. "I can't decide which I want more—to sleep for a week or take a long, hot bath."

Sergei gave me a kiss and a gentle smile, then went to the phone on a bedside table. "While you decide, I will call Kolya."

I settled for a steaming shower. There were a variety of toiletries in the drawers under the sink, along with some extra bath towels and soft flannel sheets. After rinsing out my clothes and hanging them on a towel rack to dry, I took one of the sheets, wrapped it around me sarong-style, and returned to the bedroom.

Sergei was sitting on a low bench beside the window, his face lined with fatigue, his clothes dirty and stained with blood, the computer disk in his hands.

"Is Kolya all right?" I asked quickly.

He nodded and got to his feet. "He is much relieved we are safe." The weariness left his eyes as he looked down at me.

"My clothes were filthy," I said, using practicality to cover my self-consciousness. "If you like, I'll put your jacket in some cold water while you shower."

Sergei fingered a damp strand of my hand. "You rest, *Kasenya.* I will soak the jacket."

But rest was elusive.

I sat in darkness beside the window, watching the moon and the sea. White waves running toward shore like frothy ribbons edging an ocean of deep blue silk. Gazing at the restless ebb and flow, too tired to think, too keyed up to relax, my thoughts were much like the tide, rushing, then retreating from all that had happened. . . .

The noise of the shower stopped, and my pulse quickened. An arc of light spilled across the bedroom, and I saw Sergei's broad-shouldered silhouette pause in the doorway. Then he came toward me, a towel around his hips.

"I thought you would be asleep."

I glanced away. "I guess I'm too tired. . . ."

Sergei walked back to the bathroom, then returned with a bottle of lotion. Kneeling in front of me, he poured some lotion in one hand and began warming it between his palms.

The sight of him kneeling there, dark hair damp, his naked chest bathed in moonlight, did heady things to my emotions.

"What are you doing?"

"Something my father used to do for my mother and she for him. Give me your foot."

"My foot?"

His mouth curved into a smile. "*Da*, your foot."

Feeling totally foolish, I did as he asked. Sergei took my foot between both hands and gently massaged it with the warm lotion. His touch was soothing and intimate.

"Is this an old Russian custom or something?"

He laughed softly. "Actually, the custom is more European than Russian, but one which my father was happy to adopt."

As his long fingers caressed and massaged, a sensual warmth and pleasant languour crept over me. When the silky lotion was absorbed, he poured more into his hands, and I gave him my other foot with a sigh.

Sergei raised his dark head to look at me as his hands performed their sensual massage, and I felt myself go soft and warm inside, like wax to a flame.

"I love you, *Seriozha*. . . ."

His hands grew still, and his eyes never left my face. "*Dushenka*, my feelings for you, the love. . . . In English, I lack the words."

I smiled softly, touching a hand to his dark hair. "Then tell me in Russian, *dushenka*. . . . Tell me in Russian."

There were two occupants in the rustic dining room when I entered at half past ten the next morning. An elderly couple sat at an exquisitely carved table, lingering over coffee and road maps.

"Is Mrs. Hopkins around?" I asked.

"Right here," came the cheery reply behind me.

I turned to see Doris Hopkins coming down a hall, coffee pot in hand.

This morning the braids were gone. A long pony tail tied back with a paisley scarf, hung down her back. A scarlet tee shirt and Levis made up the rest of her wardrobe.

"You're looking great this morning," she commented, pouring more coffee for the elderly couple at the table. "Sleep well?"

Hot color crept up my neck. I nodded.

"Would it be too much trouble if I took a little breakfast back to our room? My husband's still tired . . . from the accident and everything." By this time, my face felt as scarlet as her tee shirt.

Doris' dark eyes danced. "No trouble at all. Come on out to the kitchen."

Cheeks still burning, I followed her down the narrow hall.

The small kitchen was cheery and efficient, with geraniums in the window sill and a standing range with counter space in the center of the room. The woman retrieved a tray from one of the cupboards and said, "I've got some French toast, bacon and sweet rolls. How does that sound? Oh, and there's some fresh-squeezed orange juice in the fridge."

"It sounds perfect! But I . . . I hate to put you to so much trouble."

"It's no trouble. I'll just heat it up in the microwave." She gestured down the hall. "Little Josh is down for his morning nap, so I have the time."

I watched her prepare our plates and said, "You have a wonderful place here."

"Thanks. There's still a lot Carl and I want to do to fix it up, maybe add another room off the back." She took out a pitcher of chilled juice from the refrigerator. "How long have you been married?"

I glanced down. "Not long. . . ."

She poured the juice into fat green glasses, giving me an impish grin. "I hope you don't mind me saying this—I mean, I am a married woman and all, but—your Alex is something! I keep thinking I've seen him somewhere . . . on TV maybe."

My mouth went dry as I held a rigid smile.

"I know!" she said, setting the pitcher down with a thump. "It's gotta be someone on 'All My Children' or 'The Young and the Restless.'"

I nodded weakly. "People tell him that all the time. Uh, before I forget, do you know of a garage near here where we can call a tow truck?"

"There's only one. Burden's Towing in Tillamook. I'll get you the number."

"Thank you. And thanks for the breakfast. Alex will love it."

"No problem." She handed me the tray and glanced out the window. "Mist's blowing away. Looks like we're going to have a nice day."

"Yes. Yes, it does."

The man from the towing company was a little mystified at first when I told him my husband and I wouldn't be driving back to Tillamook with him. After I explained we were on our honeymoon, there were no more questions asked. Tipping back his baseball cap with a greasy hand, he gave me a wink and a toothy grin. "Can't say as I blame you. A garage ain't the kind of place I'd want to spend my honeymoon neither."

I went back to our room after the man had driven away and found Sergei standing near the window, barefoot and shirtless, wearing only Levis.

"All went well?" he asked.

I locked the door and went to his side. "Everything's fine, but the man from the garage doesn't know how long the repairs will take. Especially since it's Saturday. He might have to send to Portland for parts. Have you talked to Nikolai?"

Sergei nodded. "Kolya insists that we must not return until after dark. In daylight, the risks of being recognized by KGB or anyone else are too great."

I put both hands on his bare chest and smiled into his dark eyes. "Do you realize what that means, Mr. Alexandrov? I have an entire afternoon and evening to spend with my husband."

Sergei's mouth took mine in a long, deep kiss.

In mid-afternoon, the towing company called to tell us there was no way they could have the BMW repaired before Monday.

"We must find a way to return tonight," Sergei told me as we sat on the bed. "I have not wanted to give you added cause for concern, but I have fears for Kolya's safety."

"What kind of fears?"

"I wonder what KGB is doing during this time. What measures are being taken to find us. And I wonder what our friend Jeff Lloyd might be doing. He had much curiosity concerning you, *dushenka*. As a journalist, he might also have the means to satisfy that curiosity. I am hoping it does not lead him to your sister's house."

I clutched Sergei's hand. "What should we do?"

"There is little we can do now, but we must find a way back by tonight."

I thought a moment. "Maybe Doris will give us a ride."

"Doris?"

"The owner. She and I were talking this morning when I went down for breakfast."

Sergei smiled and shook his head. "You are a constant amazement to me, *dushenka*. So open, so giving. We walk into strange place in the middle of the night, and next morning you are friends already with the owner."

I warmed to his praise. "It's not really me. Doris is very friendly—and she thinks you look like one of her favorite 'soap' stars."

"Soap star?"

I laughed at his mystified expression. "She thinks you're very handsome. Naturally, I agreed with her."

Sergei smiled and kissed me. "Such a dutiful wife I have. Then we must work out a reasonable story for your friend Doris. It is not logical to ask for transport to your sister's house when the sister could drive here to get us."

"Why not tell her the truth—that Charlotte's out of town and we're taking care of the place. That would also explain why we don't have any luggage with us."

"Very good, *dushenka,*" he said. "You learn quickly."

Doris was more than willing to give us a ride back to Tillamook. Her duties at the inn would keep her busy until nine, she said, but after that she was free.

"Carl can take care of Josh for the evening," Doris told me when I took our breakfast dishes down to the kitchen. "It'll be a nice break to drive into town. But I'm afraid there's a problem with your room."

"A problem? I'll be happy to pay for the extra day."

"Oh, it's not that," she said quickly. "I have some folks coming from Portland. They've reserved the room for the weekend, and there aren't any other vacancies. I'm sorry."

I fought to hide my worry and disappointment. "What time do you expect them?"

"Around six. And I'll need at least an hour to get the room ready."

"I understand. Thanks, anyway."

"If you can't work out something else, I'll still be happy to drive you into Tillamook," she offered.

I nodded my thanks. "I'll talk to my husband and let you know."

Sergei was neither disappointed nor upset by the news that our room had to be vacated within the hour. "We have a way back to your sister's," he said with relief. "That is the important thing."

"But what are we going to do until then? Camp out on the beach?"

Sergei crossed to the window and gazed at the sunlit ocean. "To have a few hours with you . . . the sun on our faces, would be most pleasant," he said, a note of wistfulness in his voice.

My throat tightened as I went to his side. Sergei drew me in front of him, resting his cheek on my hair. We stood together, saying nothing, watching the endless blue roll of the waves.

"If one were searching for a Russian defector," he said thought-fully, "a logical place to find him would not be a pleasant beach in the middle of afternoon." He drew a long breath. "You have given me so much, *dushenka*. I have nothing to offer you in return . . . a few hours of walking together, enjoying the freedom of sky above us is not much to give. But it is yours, if you wish it."

I clutched his hand to my breast. Tears filled my eyes. "I wish it very much."

When Doris heard of our plan, she insisted on packing us a picnic meal.

"How far is it from here to the beach at Oceanside?" I asked, as she fed the baby his bottle from the comfort of a porch swing.

"Mmm, I'd say a good four miles. On a day like today, that's not a bad walk, but you won't feel like coming all the way back here, especially if there's a south wind blowing. I know! Why don't I pick you up at Oceanside? That way you could have the whole evening. I could meet you at the wayside parking area around nine-thirty or so."

I looked at her with a breathless smile. "Are you sure you don't mind?"

"Heavens, no. I'll be glad to." Her dark eyes took on a dreamy expression as she gazed up at the sky. "If we're lucky, there ought to be a real nice sunset tonight."

The sea wore its finest jewels that afternoon, swells of sparkling aquamarine and deepest emerald, with millions of diamonds dancing on the surface. It was Saturday and the fickle Oregon sun warmed a sky of cloudless blue. As we walked along the beach near Netarts Bay, kites of all shapes and sizes colored the sky. Sergi and I strolled past children and their fathers who held the dancing strings . . . past teenage boys playing Frisbee . . . past mothers keeping a sharp eye on little ones building sand castles. To them, we were just another couple who had come to the beach for a picnic. A mile or so beyond the bay, we left the beachgoers and tourists behind.

I watched Sergei's glance travel over the solitary stretch of beach, the forested cliffs, the blue expanse of sea. There was wonder in his eyes. Wonder and an eagerness to embrace it all. When he smiled and turned to me with the same wonder and eagerness, I threw my arms around his neck, too filled with love for him to speak. The cooler containing our lunch dropped unheeded to the sand, as Sergei pulled me close, covering my face with kisses.

The sea gave abundantly of her treasures that afternoon. Sand dollars, limpets and frilled whelk. Each discovery was presented to me, along with a kiss.

We ate in a sheltered, sandy cove, far enough away from the main beach at Oceanside to insure privacy, yet still within sight of magnificent Three Arch Rocks. Fishing boats dotted the watery horizon. Seabirds dived and soared. Above us, a trio of cormorants sang across the sky, black grace notes in the endless symphony of heaven. The tide was ebbing, and the sea was calm. There were no roaring breakers, only soft swells rolling toward shore. *Seriozha* and I sat in each other's arms, watching the waves as they curved, dipped and fell forward, lost in soft, whipped foam and dancing sunlight.

And then, almost unnoticed, the day which had seemed to stretch out forever, as endless as the ocean itself, was gone, and we were walking in silence toward the lowering sun. Three Arch Rocks loomed before us, giant black shadows rising from the sea. Behind them, the horizon burned with color—fiery vermillion, coral and gold. Overhead, a cobalt sky deepened into sapphire.

"The day's parting gift to us," Sergei said in hushed tones.

We watched, hardly moving, as golden fire spilled between the massive black monoliths and the sea licked up the flames. Even after the sun had gone, the colors refused to die. Red-orange softened to rose-pink, and the sea was mother-of-pearl. Walking along the slick, we could see the rainbow hues reflected on its smooth surface.

"Over here," I said, taking his hand and heading for Maxwell Point. "There's a place I want to show you."

Without saying anything, we walked a little faster, feeling the seconds fleeing away like the tide. Once around the rocky walls of the cliff, Sergei stared and caught his breath at the sight. Silhouetted against the rosy sky, black sea stacks sculpted by centuries of wind and water appeared as a fairy-tale castle, complete with turrets, rounded arches and pointed spires.

"*Chudesnyi. . . ,*" he breathed, putting an arm around my shoulders.

We drank in the scene in shared silence.

Later, seated on the sand, with our backs against smooth rock, we watched the sea darken and the colors fade into pale submissiveness. I tried to tell myself this moment was enough . . . that I should be grateful and not want more. But the tears came anyway, slipping silently down my face.

There was pain in Sergei's eyes as he gazed at me.

"I'm sorry," I told him, trying to smile.

"For what are you sorry?"

I swallowed a sob and the tears flowed faster. "I want more than a day . . . I don't want it to end. I want to go on sharing everything with you, doing normal, simple things. I want to love you . . . care for your house . . . have your children . . . I know I shouldn't be thinking of those things now, but I can't help it."

He was silent while I cried softly against his chest. Then he said in a strained voice. "You could have all those things . . . with your Kevin."

"I don't want Kevin! I only want you . . . ."

When he didn't speak, I raised my head and saw tears filling his dark eyes.

I put my hand to his cheek, catching the tears that fell. "I don't want to lose you, *Seriozha* . . . I can't. . . ."

We clung to each other, no longer able to hold back the pain or the tears, any more than we could hold back the changing of the tide.

"Words are faulty tools for feelings," he said at last, trying to gather control, "but there is something I wish you to remember . . . to understand. Will you try, *dushenka?*"

"I'll try. . . ."

"Rachmaninoff's 2nd Symphony . . . are you familiar with this music?"

I swallowed hard. "I don't think so."

"Of all Rachmaninoff's music, the 2nd Symphony is my favorite," he told me. "One night, when the orchestra began the third movement, something happened to me . . . inside . . . that I will never forget. I wept when I heard it. Somehow this man had created with his music the perfect expression of what love should be. Great passion, beauty and tenderness were there, and sadness also."

I looked into his eyes.

"In life, there must always be sadness, *dushenka,* to sharpen the joy," he said, gently touching my face. "As I listened, I remember thinking that I would never experience the love I was hearing in Rachmaninoff's music. That such a love belonged only to the rare few fate had chosen.

"Not long after I met Natalya, I heard the symphony again." He sighed and held me closer. "When the third movement began, the longing in me was even greater than before. Compared to what I was hearing, my love for Natalya was like a pale, sickly flower."

Sergei took my face in his hands. "Because of you, *dushenka,* I no longer need a symphony to experience love's sweetness. I will never long for it again." He smiled and kissed me. "Fate has been kind, after all. . . ."

Chapter 15

IT WAS FULLY dark when Doris Hopkins pulled onto the circular drive in front of Charlotte's home. I had some concerns at the start of the drive, how to keep a normal conversation going which would exclude Sergei as much as possible. With Doris, all it took were the typical questions one woman always seems to ask another for her to tell us full-blown episodes of her life—everything from how she met her husband, to how long she'd been in labor with little Josh.

I was happy to let her do most of the talking, as well as the driving. For one thing, it meant Sergei and I could sit close together on the front seat of the Hopkins' pick-up truck without a gear shift between us. It was heaven having him beside me in the darkness, his arm around my shoulders, his hand clutching mine. Like the sunset, the drive ended too soon, and Doris was saying warmly, "Well, I've sure enjoyed talking to you folks. Come back and see us any time."

I gave her a heartfelt hug. "Thank you. I hope we can."

Doris glanced at Sergei, an endearing look of hero-worship in her eyes. "It's been real nice meeting you."

Reaching across me, he gave her a kiss on each cheek. I saw the dazed, dreamy look in her dark eyes and discovered I could still smile after all.

Sergei and I stood, arms around each other, watching the truck's taillights disappear down the dark lane, then turned our steps toward the house.

As we entered the kitchen, I told him, "I've been thinking about what you said this afternoon—about Jeff Lloyd and the KGB finding out about this house. Maybe we shouldn't wait for Paul Miklos to get back. Maybe we should try to contact the FBI tonight."

"It is something to consider," he agreed. "We can discuss it with Kolya."

A light was on in the living room but Nikolai was not there. Sergei and I hurried up the stairs. Fear surged through me as we walked swiftly down the hall.

"Perhaps he is asleep," Sergei said, but his eyes were as worried as mine.

Nikolai lay on my nephew's bed, still wearing the rumpled clothes, his face ashen. Sergei cried out and rushed to the man's side.

"Kolya, you are ill . . . why did you not tell us?"

Nikolai shook his head weakly and reached for Sergei's hand.

I leaned over the professor, terrified by his struggle for breath, and put a hand to his forehead. My eyes met Sergei's with frightening realization. "He's burning up with fever! We've got to get him to the hospital."

"*Nyet —*"

Nikolai's protest ended in a harsh spasm of coughing. Sergei quickly put a supporting arm behind the older man's head, and I felt my own chest tighten as he struggled for breath. When the coughing subsided, I knelt beside him, clutching his hand in mine. His fingers were hot and dry to the touch.

"You have the disk?" he asked.

Sergei nodded. "Yes. There is no need to worry." He got to his feet, dark eyes meeting mine in a wordless moment of decision. We both knew what had to be done.

The sudden ringing of a phone from Mark and Charlotte's room caught my taut nerves like a trip wire. I gasped, then glanced at Sergei.

"I can't imagine who would be calling this late."

He shook his head. "Kevin . . . or your family perhaps?"

I got to my feet and ran to answer it, reaching the bedside

phone by the end of the fourth ring. Silence answered my breathless hello. Then a click, followed by the dial tone.

Sergei met me in the hall.

"Whoever it was hung up after I answered," I told him, afraid to give voice to the nagging fear inside.

A worried look crossed his face. "Kolya must have medical attention immediately."

"I know."

"Will you take him, *Kasenya?*"

I stared at him. "You're not coming?"

Sergei took both my hands in his. "Kolya will need protection, in addition to medical care. I cannot risk an arrest now. Forgive me, if I do not feel comfortable in giving the disk to your local police. There is too much at stake for it to fall into the wrong hands."

"Then we've got to reach the FBI—or someone else who can help us."

"Your police will inform the FBI once you have taken Kolya to hospital."

"*Seriozha —*"

"I will wait here, *dushenka.* I must. Please, go now."

The sound of Nikolai's heavy coughing added urgency to his words.

"At least let me call Kevin's father. We may need his help."

Sergei drew a tense breath. "If you feel it is wise, call him. I will assist Kolya to the car."

Grant Barlow's deep voice answered the phone, barely getting out, "Why, Cassie, this is a nice surprise —" before I cut him off with, "I'm sorry to be calling so late, but I need your help."

"You know I'll be glad to help if I can," he said smoothly.

"I don't have time to explain everything on the phone, but some friends of mine are in serious trouble, and they —"

"Are you all right?" he broke in.

"Yes, I'm fine, but I can't talk right now. How long will it take you to get to the hospital in Tillamook?"

"If I drive, I can be there in a little over an hour."

"Thanks. I'll meet you there."

"Cassie —"

I hung up the phone as Sergei entered the kitchen with Nikolai, a supporting arm around the older man's shoulders. Nikolai's breathing was rapid and shallow. He barely had the strength to walk. I rushed to his side, taking his arm in a firm grip. My mind and senses swam with *deja vu.* Suddenly, it was that first night all over again. A tall man and I were dragging a stocky man's exhausted weight across the sand, struggling up steep, cliffside steps, with the roar of the dark sea below us. . . .

As we inched our way into the garage toward the car, I felt the scene shift back to now. The urgency and danger of that first night had not changed . . . but these men were no longer strangers thrust into my life. These men were my life.

Once Nikolai was settled on the front seat, Sergei followed me around to the driver's side, then pulled me into his arms, pressing my face close to his. "Be very careful, *dushenka.*"

"I will. I'll try to call you from the hospital."

"Two rings, then hang up," he reminded me, worry edging his voice.

"I love you. . . ."

His answer was in Russian, followed by a hard kiss.

As I got into the car, Nikolai turned his gaze toward Sergei and lifted a hand. *"Do svidaniya, Seriozha . . .*my friend."

Sergei leaned down and gave the older man a smile. "No, Kolya . . . there will be no good-byes between us. I will see you soon."

Nikolai sighed and leaned back against the seat.

Sergei touched a hand to my cheek, whispering in English for the first time, "I love you, Cassandra."

I sat in a hard plastic chair outside Nikolai's hospital room, staring at oatmeal-colored walls and wondering how long it would be before Kevin's father arrived. Seated around me were an impressive assortment of blue and tan uniforms: Deputy Sheriff Cal Jeppson of the County Sheriff's office, Walt Stoker from the State Police, and Officer Kendall Smith from the Tillamook Police

Department. Nearby, Sheriff Gene Dayley stood talking with another police office. The past hour or more had been a blur of questions, admittance forms, permission for treatment forms, police reports and settling the confusing matter of proper jurisdiction.

My glance shifted to the closed door of Nikolai's room with its warning sign of No Smoking, Oxygen in Use, then to the nurses' station where a green-clad doctor was conferring with one of the nurses, then to the elevators at the end of the hallway. Where was Kevin's father? A Dr. Merrill was in with Nikolai. Why wasn't he coming out? It seemed like days instead of minutes since the slender, soft-spoken physician had gone into the room.

I realized then that one of the police officers had spoken to me. I turned to meet Walt Stoker's penetrating blue eyes.

"I'm sorry. What did you say?"

"I'd like to clarify a few more details of your story," he said. "You haven't given us much to go on here—just that you found Mr. Petrovsky on Wednesday night and helped him to your grandfather's place. That was three days ago. Why didn't you call the police?"

"He asked me not to."

Walt Stoker looked at me with a long sigh.

Deputy Cal Jeppson tapped impatient fingers on the arm of his chair, then ran a hand through his thinning hair. "You really don't expect us to buy that, do you, Miss Graves? Some Russian shows up at your grandfather's place, asks you not to call the police, and you agree—just like that."

I met his skeptical glance with a sigh as weary as Walt Stokers. "I'm not asking you to buy anything, Deputy Jeppson—and we've been through this before."

"Then you still say you don't know anything about his companion. . . ." Jeppson frowned at his notes. "Ser-jee Alexander?"

I had to stop myself from correcting his pathetic pronunciation. "I'm sorry, I can't answer that."

"Miss Graves, are you aware that Mr. Alexandrov's wanted for murder," Walt Stoker inserted quietly.

"I'd heard something about that, yes."

The state patrol officer leaned forward, his blue eyes serious on my face. "Miss Graves, whatever reasons you may have for wanting to protect this man, you'd be wise to let the proper authorities handle it."

I gave him an apologetic look and said nothing. Throughout the questioning, Walt Stoker had been nothing but polite, in spite of my fragmentary story and refusal to answer questions. As the minutes wore on, Deputy Jeppson's impatience was becoming more evident. So was Officer Smith's, but there was little he could do about it, since the case was out of his jurisdiction. The city police were cooperating with the County Sheriff's Office and the State Police in providing protection for Nikolai while he was at the hospital, but other than that, it wasn't his affair. Legs stretched out in front of him, back horizontal against the hard chair, he was ready to call it a night.

I glanced at the clock again, wishing I could call *Seriozha,* wondering how he was, wanting him with me. . . .

The door to Nikolai's room opened, and I was instantly on my feet.

I tried to read something from the doctor's impassive features, not sure if I saw worry or fatigue in his eyes. "Dr. Merrill . . . how is he?"

"Mr. Petrovsky's condition is guarded," he answered. "Since the pneumonia is viral, antibiotics won't be of much help. We're treating the fever, of course, and administering oxygen therapy."

Is he going to be all right?"

"We won't know for a while." A flicker of compassion warmed his eyes as he looked at me. "But I hope so."

The thread of doubt in his voice cut through me. "Can I see him?"

"Not for a few minutes. The nurse is with him now."

"Cassie?"

I turned slowly, feeling an oppressive heaviness inside and saw Grant Barlow striding down the hall, briefcase in hand. Even in a golf shirt and casual slacks, he looked every inch the attorney. Walking beside him, anxious blue eyes seeking mine, was Kevin.

Kevin stood back as his father walked confidently into the circle of uniforms. "I'm Miss Graves' attorney, Grant Barlow. We'll need some place to talk—in private."

"There's a doctor's lounge down the hall," Dr. Merrill said. "I don't believe anyone's there right now."

"That'll be fine."

When Kevin came toward me, extending a comforting arm, I stepped back automatically, my glance sliding away from his.

"I don't know that it's necessary for Miss Graves to have two attorneys present," Deputy Jeppson inserted, giving Kevin a pointed look.

Grant Barlow fixed the deputy with one of his withering courtroom stares. "This is my son, Kevin, Miss Graves' fiance. I don't see see why his presence should be a problem, but if you prefer, he can wait here while I talk with Cassie."

I almost smiled as the Deputy shrugged and stepped back. Grant Barlow was a middle-aged man of average height and build with average looks—graying hair and pleasant features, a little on the sharp side—but somehow, one never noticed that. The moment he entered a room, his confident, commanding personality was instantly felt. Physically, Kevin's handsome face and muscular six-foot build were more imposing, yet even he seemed to shrink in stature whenever the two were together.

The doctor's lounge was more like a large closet, furnished with a couch, two chairs and a cot. A table with a coffee urn, cups and a hot plate was squeezed against one wall.

After ushering us inside, Dr. Merrill tactfully retreated, telling me in his soft-spoken voice, "I'll let you know if there's any change in Mr. Petrovsky's condition."

Kevin took me in his arms the moment he was gone. "Cass, I've been worried out of my mind. My God, what's been going on? I've called and called. . . ."

I let him hold me, feeling strangely wooden and stiff, where once I had been comfortably familiar. "I'm sorry, Kevin. I knew you'd be worried, but there wasn't anything I could do. . . ."

When he released me, I turned to his father and gave him a grateful hug. "Thank you for coming."

Grant Barlow's arms were reassuring. So was his robust, no-nonsense voice as he led me to the couch. "All right, my girl. Let's hear about this fix you've gotten yourself into. And I don't mind telling you, my curiosity is at a peak."

The telling took over an hour. The only things I omitted were my feelings for Sergei and the location of his whereabouts. As we talked, I kept most of my attention focused on Kevin's father. His questions were intelligent and straightforward, his comments few. If he was shocked or critical of what I had done, he hid it well.

Sitting beside me on the couch, Kevin said little, but I could sense the subtle shift of his emotions from shock and concern, to sharp hurt and anger. Even when I wasn't looking at him, I could feel the growing heat of his frustration.

"Is there anything you can do to help them?" I said finally.

Grant Barlow answered without hesitation. "For the moment, I think Dr. Petrovsky is in good hands, but we need to get your friend Sergei some protection as soon as possible."

Relief mixed with fear made my voice breathless and unsteady. "Can you keep the Soviets away from him?"

"I'm not sure. Since Alexandrov is still a Soviet citizen, their government representatives do have the right to assure themselves that he's well and not being coerced."

"Even if those representatives are KGB?"

Kevin's father gave me a sympathetic look. "I understand your concerns, Cassie, but it's important to establish that he acted independently—on his own. That's where I come in. But there's no way I can give him the kind of protection he'll need. Did you say the police have already called the FBI's office in Portland?"

"Yes."

"But you haven't said anything to the local authorities about Alexandrov or the computer disk."

"No."

Grant Barlow frowned and rubbed his temples. "We may have a problem."

"What kind of problem?"

"Nothing we can't work out," he reassured me, giving my knee a comforting pat. "I was just thinking that since the FBI don't know anything about your friend, they might not feel any great urgency to get an agent out here in the middle of the night. To their way of thinking, Dr. Petrovsky is just a Soviet scientist who wants to defect, not some important government official or someone with sensitive information that the Soviets are desperate to get back. How sure are you that Alexandrov is safe where he is now?"

Fear tightened my throat. I could only shake my head. Kevin was staring at me again, with an expression that bordered on suspicion.

Grant Barlow got to his feet. "I think the first thing we'd better do is find out when the FBI will be here and get this Alexandrov to a safe house where he can meet with them." He helped himself to some coffee in a paper cup and stood, brows furrowed in thought, sipping the hot liquid.

In a strained voice, Kevin asked, "Can I get you some coffee?"

I shook my head. "Not right now."

"The beach house at Cape Meares might be a good place." Grant Barlow looked at me, and I gave him a shaky smile. "And Cassie, I think it'd be best if I picked up Alexandrov and drove him there. You've done more than enough for the man," he said quietly, adding, "You and Kevin can meet us there later, if you like."

I stood up and put a hand on his arm. "I understand what you're saying, but *Seriozha* doesn't know you —"

"Cass, you heard what Dad said. You've done enough." Kevin got to his feet and turned me to face him. "I want you to stay here with me, where I know you'll be safe."

"I'm sorry, but I have to go. . . ."

"You don't *have* to go! What's got into you, Cass?"

Grant Barlow tossed away his paper cup and moved to the door. "Why don't I let you two discuss this. I'll see if I can find out what time the FBI will be here."

Kevin faced me in cold, silent anger, his hands gripping my arms. He drew a deep breath, trying to gather some control. "All right, Cass, what's going on?"

"You know what's going on —"

"No, I don't. I don't understand any of this. Especially you. All I know is you're so caught up playing mother hen for two Russians that you won't listen to reason!"

I stood there, shaking with emotion, trying to remain in control.

There was a tense moment of silence, then he sighed.

"Cass, I'm sorry to blow up at you like that—but can't you see, it's because I love you? I've been worried sick about you. Why else do you think I dropped everything and flew back from New York?"

There was nothing I could say to him. His mouth tightened, and he let go my arms. "I don't understand you, Cass."

I tentatively touched his arm. "I know. . . ."

There was a light knock on the door, then Grant Barlow entered. "The FBI should be here within the hour. One of us'll need to stay here and give them directions to the house."

"You and Kevin can work that out. I'll meet you at the beach house in say, half an hour or so."

Kevin stiffened beside me as I met his father's questioning look of concern.

"Cassie, I'm sure you have your reasons for wanting to do this, but I have to tell you I don't feel it's wise. I wish you'd reconsider."

"I'm sorry, Grant. I appreciate your concern, but I know what I'm doing. Am I free to go or do I have to check with the police?"

"No, you're free to go."

"Thanks again . . . for everything." I kissed his cheek and smiled into his worried eyes. "Please don't worry about me. I'll see you out at the beach house."

Kevin followed close at my heels as I left the lounge and walked down the hall toward Nikolai's room. Deputy Jeppson and another officer were stationed outside the door. As I approached, a heavy-set nurse with a scrubbed pink face was just leaving.

"Is it all right if I see Dr. Petrovsky now?" I asked her.

"Dr. Petrovsky's not allowed visitors," she said firmly.

"I know, but I'm the one who brought him to the hospital. I won't stay long."

"He's sleeping," she said in a tone as final as a shut door.

"I won't wake him . . . I just want to see him . . . that's all. . . ."

The look in my eyes must have communicated more than my

faltering words, because she gave a grudging sigh and stepped aside.

I glanced at Kevin.

"I'll wait for you here," he said, his voice gentler than I'd heard all night.

I stood just inside the door, staring at the figure on the bed. Kolya's eyes were closed. His big chest labored for air, caving inward with each breath, in spite of the oxygen mask covering his mouth and nose. The sound of his short, rasping breaths was nearly smothered by the oxygen's loud, steady hiss and the high-pitched beep of monitoring machines.

My mind saw a picture of him standing beside the garage, with Gulliver in his arms, as Sergei and I drove away. I could still hear his parting words.

"May God keep you safe," I whispered in return, tears moistening my eyes, then left the room.

Kevin took my arm as I walked woodenly down the hall toward the elevators.

"Look, Cass . . . if you still insist on doing this, at least let me go with you. Dad can stay here and talk to the FBI when they arrive."

I pressed the Down button and gave him an apologetic smile. "Kevin, I have to go alone."

"But why —"

We got into the elevator and the two nurses there saved me from having to answer. I stared straight ahead at the heavy metal doors, avoiding Kevin's glance. Why indeed? There was no logical reason why he shouldn't come with me. Except for the fact that Kevin's presence meant I wouldn't have any time alone with *Seriozha.*

We left the elevator and entered the waiting area of the Emergency Room, Kevin still holding my arm in a tense grip. My emotions were in a turmoil, worrying about Nikolai's condition, hoping Sergei was still safe at the Kilchis house and wondering how I could tactfully tell my fiance to get lost.

"Cass, you still haven't given me an answer," Kevin was saying with ragged patience. "I just don't feel right about you going alone!"

The sliding glass doors parted with an electronic shudder. We stepped into an area where there were several vending machines, and two cubicles containing pay phones. I turned my head to answer Kevin at the same time a man using one of the phones glanced our way. A jolt of recognition went through me carrying the force of an electric shock. Then we were through the second set of sliding glass doors and outside.

Still reeling from shock, I ran to my car. I couldn't think. I couldn't talk. All I knew was that I had to get away.

"Cass, what's wrong with you?"

I tossed a frightened glance toward the Emergency Room Entrance but Jeff Lloyd hadn't followed.

I fumbled in my jacket pocket for the car keys, then climbed into the Honda.

"Cassie?"

I looked up at my fiance's bewildered face, and all I could say was, "I'm sorry, Kevin."

I backed out of the parking space with a roar, leaving him standing there alone.

Chapter 16

I WAS HALFWAY to Charlotte's before I had enough presence of mind to realize how stupid I had been. I should have told Kevin about Jeff Lloyd. I should have alerted Grant. Or the police. Instead, I had run like a terrified rabbit pursued by a pack of hounds. How did Lloyd find out about Nikolai so quickly? And if he knew, did that mean the KGB was also close at hand?

Fear kept fatigue far from me. I fairly flew up the winding Kilchis road and across the dark fields to my sister's home. Gunning up the drive, I grabbed the automatic opener off the seat and gave it two quick clicks. Before the heavy door had risen even half way, Sergei was ducking under it and running toward the car.

"Replace the door and turn off your lights!" he ordered in a hiss.

"What — ?"

"The door! Make it to go down. Quickly!" He ran around the car and climbed in beside me while I did as he asked.

"Seriozha, what's wrong?"

"Is there another road—a different way for us to leave?"

Eyes wide, I glanced past the line of trees, searching the darkness of the sloping lane below.

"They are driving without lights," he said, answering my unspoken question. Then, with increased urgency. *"Kasenya,* is there another way?"

I nodded and backed the car around.

The road was little more than a cow track across the pastures above Mark and Charlotte's home. During the rainy reason, it turned into a soft sea of mud that was totally impassable. But now, the road was hard as baked clay. I gripped the wheel white-knuckled as we jolted across the dark fields toward the main highway, while Sergei kept anxious watch behind us.

A wire fence barring cows from an old bridge crossing the Kilchis nearly barred our passage as well. Sergei was out of the car and running toward the fence before we could brake to a complete stop.

I put a hand to my mouth, praying the gate wasn't locked, and glanced behind us. Black trees hid the home from my view, but I knew they were there.

It seemed forever before the gate swung open in front of him. The Honda creaked across the bridge, groaned up a weed-choked embankment, then bit into hard asphalt and roared down the Kilchis road.

"Jeff Lloyd was at the hospital," I said.

"He saw you?"

"Yes, but he didn't follow me. I'm sure of that."

"There was no need," Sergei answered. "A phone call is all it would take for others to follow."

I shuddered with the realization. "Do you think we're being followed now?"

His quiet, "Not yet," gave little reassurance.

As we drove past the hospital, Sergei turned his head to stare at the large brick building.

"Kolya has pneumonia," I said.

He nodded, not speaking.

I had turned onto Bay Ocean Road and the dark waters of the bay were in view before Sergei asked as if it were the last thing that mattered, "Where are we going?"

"Somewhere safe," I said, silently praying it was true.

The moon hung low in the western sky, and the rushing voice of the sea welcomed us to the quiet little community huddled at land's end. Dawn was still hours away, and most of Cape Meares' houses were completely dark. Only a few street lights alleviated the blackness as I drove along the dead end road to the Barlow's home.

"The FBI will meet us here?" Sergei asked.

"Yes. Kevin's family have a house at the end of this street, and they —" I broke off and swore under my breath.

Directly ahead, a red Mazda was parked beside a dark frame house. Lights glowed softly from the windows and smoke curled from the stone chimney upwards into the night.

Sergei gave me a sharp look. "KGB — ?"

I let out a long sigh. "No. Kevin."

The rustic brown house stood on the corner of Fourth and Pacific. Beyond it, the asphalt road changed to gravel and led to a few hillside residences. To the right, Pacific Street ran straight for another hundred and fifty yards, before the rocky hillside tumbled down to the sea.

Sergei gave me a curious look, but said nothing when I turned right and drove past the Barlow's beach house. I parked the Honda near two large boulders at the end of the street, switched off the engine and sat staring at the ocean.

High tide sent dark waves crashing toward the rocky shore. We could hear the hollow tumbling of the rocks, as the waves pulled them restlessly out to sea, then pushed them back again. A mile offshore, Pyramid Rock rose from the ocean like a giant dorsal fin.

"I love the ocean at night," I said. "Somehow, it's even more powerful. It frightens me, but I love it."

Moonlight fell softly on Sergei's face as I turned to him, pleading with my eyes: Don't ask me to explain. Just hold me.

Desperation added frenzied sweetness to our kisses. My hands dug into his back, pulling him closer still. Below us, waves crashed and rolled. Sea thunder roared its powerful music and passion had its way.

Kevin was sitting in front of the fireplace when Sergei and I walked in the back door. He got to his feet, then stood, staring at the two of us, as we entered the room.

I had a sudden picture of what he must be seeing. My hair,

disheveled. My mouth bare, with lips slightly swollen. Cheeks glowing. Eyes naked with love.

Kevin's mouth parted, then tightened, as his stunned gaze slid from me to Sergei.

"Kevin, this is Sergei. . . ."

He gave a slight nod, but his hands remained in his pockets. "Sit down. I'll — uh, add some more wood to the fire."

Three fat logs were already burning in the big stone fireplace, but Kevin took two more from the wood box near the hearth and added them to the blaze.

Sergei glanced around the large, rustic room, smiled at me with his eyes, then sat down on the couch. I sat beside him, which left a large rocking chair for Kevin.

"Will your father be here soon?" I asked.

"Should be." He glanced at his watch, then looked at me again, his eyes puzzled and probing. "Would you like some coffee or something?"

"No thanks."

"You must be exhausted. If you want to lie down for a few minutes —"

I shook my head, feeling a surge of anger that his questions and concern excluded Sergei.

Kevin cleared his throat and brushed a smudge of dirt from his shoe. Fixing Sergei with a stiff smile, he said, "So . . . Cassie tells me you've had quite the adventure the past few days."

I groaned inwardly. "You know, I think maybe some coffee would be nice. It's been a long night."

Kevin got to his feet. "I've got some in the kitchen. Do you want to — ?"

"Thanks. I'll show Sergei around the house while you get it ready."

There wasn't a lot to show, but I desperately needed something to do. Other than the large main room and small kitchen, there were three bedrooms and a bath. Kevin was always apologetic about the cabin's simple furnishings and rustic appearance and made a point of telling me that someday the entire place was going to be repaired and remodeled. Secretly, I hoped that someday never happened. I loved the old wooden floors, the raftered ceiling and the comfortable, make-piece decorating . . . the 'Aunt Jemima' cookie jar in the kitchen and cupboard doors that had minds of their own . . . the space heaters which either worked wonderfully or refused to function . . . the small-paned windows that were painted shut. And the outside door near the fireplace that was rarely used because a pair of swallows had made their nest on the ledge above it. They were all part of the cabin's charm and unique personality.

Sergei gave me a smiling, sympathetic glance as we returned to the living room. I met his dark eyes, needing to kiss him more than I needed to breathe, and painfully aware of Kevin's watchful gaze from the kitchen.

From outside, we heard a car's approach, then voices. I released a thankful sigh and pressed Sergei's hand. "Thank heaven. They're finally here."

From the kitchen doorway, I could see Kevin, as he left the counter to answer a knock on the back door. He stood for a moment, with his back to us, talking to someone outside, then stood aside.

Two men entered, wearing casual clothes and windbreakers. Kevin shook each of their hands and ushered them into the living room.

"Cassie, this is Agent Bob Edmunds and Mike Smith."

Agent Edmunds was medium height, thirtyish, with light brown hair and deep-set eyes. His slender, muscular build was set off by a snug blue golf shirt and dark slacks. The handshake he gave me was firm and reassuring.

Mike Smith was taller, nearly six feet. His dark hair carried a hint of gray, and his rangy build was lean and fit. High cheekbones and an olive complexion set off his chiseled features and dark eyes. The nod he gave me was respectfully reserved.

Sergei stood beside me as Kevin made the instructions, which failed to include him. Offering his hand, he said with quiet dignity, "Sergei Andreievich Alexandrov."

Agent Edmunds stepped toward him with a smile. "Mr. Alexandrov. . . ."

I glanced toward the back door, surprised that Kevin's father hadn't accompanied them. "Where's Mr. Barlow? I thought he'd be coming with you."

"He'll be arriving shortly," Edmunds answered. "In another car."

"Have a seat," Kevin invited, gesturing to the couch. "Can I get you some coffee? We were just about to have some when you came."

"Thank you, no," Edmunds answered politely. "We won't be staying."

I stared at him. "Not staying?"

"We were sent to accompany Mr. Alexandrov to a safe house."

"I thought we were meeting here. . . ."

"The plans have been altered to insure Mr. Alexandrov's safety," Edmunds explained. "And for your protection as well. I'm sorry, but we'll need to leave right away."

"Oh . . . Well, I'll get my jacket and —"

"That won't be necessary, Miss Graves."

I caught his meaning and felt my world drop out from under me. Sergei was going. Now. I looked at him, not knowing what to say, my heart beating in hard, painful strokes.

"I'm sorry, but we really must go," Edmunds said quietly, putting a hand to Sergei's elbow.

Seriozha reached out, gently touching my face. "*Do svidaniya, dushenka. . . .*"

Hot tears sprang to my eyes, then spilled down my cheeks. I tried to say his name, and it ended in a tight sob.

Agent Smith produced a handkerchief from his pocket and offered it to me. I reached out blindly to take it and found myself staring at the heavy gold ring on his left hand. I stood very still, mind reeling, the blood pounding through my veins.

I took the handkerchief and wiped my eyes. "Would it be all right if I had just a moment to say good-bye . . . please?" Not waiting for their answer, I took Sergei's hand and led him to a far corner of the room beyond the fireplace.

Edmunds and Smith stood passively watching near the doorway to the kitchen. Kevin's face was a white mask of hurt and anger.

I put my arms around Sergei's neck, murmuring against his mouth, "The ring . . . they're KGB. . . ." Sergei's arms tensed only slightly as he held me. Our lips parted long enough for me to whisper. "The door. . ." then I kissed him again.

The next moment, I stepped back and Sergei bolted for the door.

Edmunds shouted something and shoved Kevin aside. Smith was right behind him. The two men lunged past me for the open door, but it was too late. *Seriozha* was gone. . . .

Kevin rushed up to me with an incredulous look. "What the hell do you think you're doing?"

I smiled at him, sank down on a chair and started to cry.

Not five minutes later, two cars pulled up beside the beach house, and I heard Grant Barlow's booming voice. He entered the kitchen with two men following behind.

Kevin's father took in my tear-streaked face, then glanced around the living room. "What's happened? Where's Alexandrov?"

"He ran away," Kevin said, shaking his head. "Bolted out of here a few minutes ago with two FBI agents on his tail."

"They weren't FBI," I said. "They were the same men who broke into the cottage the other night."

Grant Barlow stared at me. "Are you sure? I thought you said you didn't get a good look at them."

"When one of them grabbed the car window, I saw his ring."

A bearded man with intense blue eyes came forward and asked, "What were these agents' names?"

"Bob Edmunds and Mike Smith."

The bearded man produced a small leather case from his raincoat and showed me the identification inside. Beside me, I heard Kevin's startled breath as he glanced at the name.

"How long did you say they've been gone?" Agent Edmunds asked tensely.

"Only a few minutes."

"Does Alexandrov have the disk?"

"Yes."

Edmunds turned and ran from the room. His companion had already gone.

Grant Barlow put a comforting arm around my shoulders. "Don't worry. They'll find him."

I sat, staring into the flames.

Gray dawn approached, bringing a fine gray mist from the sea. The eastern sky was bleak, with no hint of sun, and the forested slopes of Cape Meares wore a gauzy shroud. I stood on the road above the beach house, staring at the hillside where the search for Sergei still continued.

Darkness had hindered authorities' efforts for almost two hours, but now FBI agents, local police and the Coast Guard were combing the area both north and south of Cape Meares.

"Cassie. . . ?"

Kevin's voice called to me from the doorway of the beach house.

"You need some rest, darling. Come inside."

I shook my head, feeling the endearment cut through me. "I can't rest."

"Come inside, anyway. It's too cold and wet out for you to be standing out here."

From the north, a low throbbing could be heard in the distance. I stopped, searching the gray skies. As the throbbing grew louder, I spotted a Coast Guard helicopter, flying south along the coastline. Kevin left the doorway to peer at the sky.

As we watched, the helicopter altered its course along the beach to circle the mist-shrouded slopes and forests of the cape.

I caught my breath and started running down the street.

"Cassie! Where're you going?"

Kevin ran after me and grabbed my arm.

"They've found him! I know they have."

"You don't know that."

"Let me go, Kevin."

"Cassie, there's nothing you can do."

"Maybe not, but I can't stand just sitting here waiting."

"Then I'll go with you."

The helicopter was enveloped in mist, but I could still hear the whir of the rotors as we headed south along the beach toward the cape. The smell of salt was strong on the air, and gulls were gathered on the slick. A smooth stretch of beach that had been underwater only hours before, was now exposed by the outgoing tide. Straight ahead I could see the tide pools and a slippery maze of boulders covered with seaweed and barnacles. Crossing them was an intricate test of balance and judgment, which at times could prove treacherous. Kevin followed, frowning and silent, as I clambered over the rocks and around tide pools where jeweled anemones quivered in the clear water and starfish clung to the crevices.

Not far beyond the rocks was a secluded cove and sea caves hollowed out of the cape's rocky sides. I was breathless and sweating by the time we reached it, in spite of the morning chill. Storms and tides had tossed huge driftwood logs like playthings, far up into the rocky cove. I walked among them, eyes searching the cliffs and forests above, ears straining for the sound of the helicopter. All I could hear was the rushing voice of the sea.

"*Seriozha . . . Seriozha!*"

The sea caves carried his name to the waves in a strange, hollow echo, but the sea gave no answer.

Kevin stood watching me, shoulders hunched, hands huddled in his pockets and sadness in his eyes.

I turned without a word and began walking back through the mist.

Soft rain was falling by the time we trudged up the street. I glanced through the rain toward the brown house on the corner, suddenly realizing all the cars were gone except for Kevin's red Mazda. I caught my breath, then broke into a run.

Grant Barlow caught me in his arms as I burst into the house. "It's all right, honey. He's safe."

"Thank God. . . ." My voice broke and I turned toward the living room, but Kevin's father still held me.

"Sergei's safe, but he's not here," he said quietly.

I felt a cold heaviness inside. "Where is he?"

Chapter 17

THREE WEEKS PASSED. Three weeks of wondering, waiting, knowing only that Sergei was alive . . . somewhere.

I couldn't go back to the cottage. Something in me wasn't ready to face that yet. Mom and Dad suggested that I move home for a while until "things" were settled, and I was glad to do so. Kevin was kind, patient and made no demands. His kindness couldn't conceal the hurt I saw in his eyes and only increased my guilt for causing him such pain.

Mark not only forgave me for taking his "baby," but managed to milk it for all it was worth. His car was now a legend—the black BMW that outwitted the KGB. His and Charlotte's home became a scenic landmark for miles around, with Bryan and Peter giving guided tours of their bedrooms to wide-eyed friends. The *place* where those Russians stayed. Mrs. Davis basked in her newfound notoriety. She wasn't the least bit angry about my deception, only disappointed that Sergei and Nikolai wouldn't be coming over for dinner. And when I introduced her to Kevin, she was positively chilly.

Grant Barlow kept me up to date with the latest legal developments in the case and whatever other information he was permitted to give. I learned much during that time about everything except what I wanted to know most: Would I see *Seriozha* again? Was he thinking of me? Did he still love me. . . .

At night, I would lie awake, thinking about all that had happened. At times, it seemed as if the past had never been . . . and the future never coming. Only this strange limbo existence of waiting.

My meetings with the FBI and other authorities brought startling facts to light. Fragments of information, painstakingly pieced together, gradually formed a fascinating mosaic of intrigue.

Jeffrey Arthur Lloyd, III, was a legitimate journalist working for the *Tribune*, who also made regular contributions to *Novosti Press Agency,* the publishing arm of the KGB. The son of a prominent banker, Lloyd had been recruited by a prowling KGB/ diplomat from the Consulate while he was attending Stanford University several years before and had been perfecting his "disinformation" skills ever since. Lloyd's name was on the disk, along with the dates of meetings and hand-offs to various Soviets. It was Jeff Lloyd who discovered the Kilchis house and called the KGB. After seeing me at the hospital, he had waited there, hoping to learn more. Kevin had unknowingly led him to the house at Cape Meares.

In a desperate attempt to recover the disk, Grigor Markevich sent Vladimir Rusak and Valeri Smirnov to the house. It was Rusak, acting under Markevich's orders, who was responsible for Yelena's death.

I was never told much about the contents of the disk, which in a way, told me a great deal about its importance. The FBI assured me that the information was more than enough to send Comrade Markevich home to Moscow.

Late one August afternoon, Kevin asked if I could drop by his father's law office for a few minutes. I went, expecting no more than a social call and perhaps another crumb of information. Instead, I found Agent Bob Edmunds. He greeted me with his usual warmth and firm handshake, but something in his eyes started my heart pounding like a trip-hammer.

"I know this has been a difficult time for you," he began as Kevin and I sat down on a plush leather couch, "and I want you to know how much I appreciate your patience and cooperation the past few weeks." Taking a chair opposite me, he smiled and said, "Now that it's official, I thought you'd like to know Petrovsky and Alexandrov have been granted political asylum and full protection by the government."

I leaned back, savoring the news with a sigh. "Where are they? Can you tell me?"

"For the present, Dr. Petrovsky is staying with a member of the State Department. He's been offered a teaching position at an oceanographic institute back east. That's all I can say." The man's simple pause seemed to stretch into an endless gulf of silence before he added, "Alexandrov will be continuing his work in marine biology. In fact, he's leaving soon for a lengthy expedition in the north Pacific."

I moistened my lips. "How soon?"

Bob Edmunds frowned and flipped through his notebook. "Sometime this week, I think. Yes, here it is. His ship leaves from Astoria this evening."

Kevin caught up with me as I rushed from the building.

"Did you know?" I choked. "Did you know he was leaving today?"

His silence told me that he did.

"Why didn't you tell me? Kevin, how could you do this?"

"I haven't done anything, Cass. If he'd wanted you to know, Alexandrov could have told you himself."

"I don't believe that."

"It's true."

We stood beside his car, with the ripe August sun beating down on us. Inside, I felt as gray and lifeless as that last morning in Cape Meares.

"It's time you got him out of your system, Cass. There's no future for you with Sergei. He knows that. I think he's always known it. Now you've got to face it whether you like it or not." He drew a long breath. "Come on. I'll drive you to Astoria."

We drove along the Columbia toward the lowering sun. I didn't say a word to Kevin the entire time. My throat ached, and there was a tightness in my chest that seemed to grow stronger with every breath.

When we reached the dock, I saw a large ship alongside the wharf.

"Hurry, Kevin. . . ."

The gang plank had been removed and line men were already tossing away the heavy ropes which held the ship to its mooring, as Kevin parked the car. I was out and running down the street toward the wharf before he switched off the engine.

One of the line men, swarthy and wrinkled, with a grimy plaid shirt and a knit cap on his head, glanced at me with a flicker of sympathy. "Sorry, Miss. It's too late to board her."

I walked quickly past him, not answering. There were a few others on the dock, but I scarcely saw them.

The crew and passengers were on deck, leaning over the rails, taking their last look at land. Gulls were wheeling around the ship, their wings catching the sun's parting gold.

Standing on the edge of the dock, I searched the faces.

"Seriozha. . . ."

He couldn't have heard the faint, breathless sound, but his dark eyes found me, and I saw his mouth curve into a beautiful, sad smile.

The ship eased away from the dock almost soundlessly, and the Columbia took her into its broad, watery path. I walked along the edge of the wharf with the ship as she left, until I could go no farther. The water shone blue and gold. The sky was rose and gold. The breeze blowing around me seemed to carry away the strong dock smells of creosote and oily timbers, leaving only the fresh, salt tang of the sea. Above me, gulls wheeled and cried. Seriozha raised his hand in silent farewell across the watery distance which separated us, and I offered him mine.

Soon his ship was only a small dark object in a river of shining gold. Then she was gone.

September came, bringing mild, windless days. I remained in Eugene with my parents, miles from the sea, but I knew all the same that the ocean would be jewel-colored, deepest emerald and aquamarine, and I ached with memories.

Kevin refused to take back his ring, even though I couldn't bring myself to wear it, and insisted all I needed was time. One weekend in late October, he dropped by my parents' home unannounced with flowers and a pleased, secretive smile.

"What's the occasion?"

"We're going out tonight. Why don't you wear your black velvet dress. It's one of my favorites."

"Where are we going?"

He smiled again. "It's a surprise. But I think it's something you'll like."

That evening when we pulled up in front of the civic auditorium in Portland, I turned to him and said, "You're right. I am surprised."

Kevin had a one-word description for all classical music—boring. The few times we had gone to concerts, he'd been restless or nodding off throughout the program.

"You've seemed a little down lately," he said by way of explanation. "I thought this would give you a lift."

Kevin handed me the program as we took our seats in the spacious hall, and I definitely got a "lift."

"Is something wrong?" he asked, looking at my face.

I shook my head and clutched the program which featured Rachmaninoff's 2nd Symphony and told him, "No—everything's fine."

I sat in restless anticipation during a Rossini overature and some Debussy nocturnes. The intermission was noisy, annoying, endless. As we took our seats once more, Kevin turned to me with a pleased smile.

"I'm glad you're happy with my little surprise. I haven't seen that sparkle in your eyes for months."

I straightened my skirt, picked up the program and leaned back in the plush seat. The conductor made his entrance, acknowledged the applause with a dignified bow, then turned to the orchestra.

The music began, somber and dark, like a Russian winter with no hope of sun.

Kevin covered a yawn and settled back in his seat.

Then, with a trembling rush, the music began to build, bursting into a melody that promised all the richness of spring. Its beauty and sadness, its pure Russianness, sent tears slipping silently down my cheeks. The music brought them back to me . . . Sergei and Nikolai. I saw glasses clinking in a golden haze and heard their voices offering the simple toast, "to peace and friendship."

As the music soared, I thought of that first night at the cottage when I had rejected Rachmaninoff's music, afraid of its passion. Now I let it take me, opening my heart to every phrase, reveling in the pain as well as the sweetness.

The first movement ended in a burst of brilliant color, and the second began in a frenzied tempo of anticipation. The sudden burst of volume roused Kevin, and he sat up with a start. Blinking, he shifted position, then stared at the orchestra with practiced concentration.

The waiting was sweet torture. One moment, the music died down, and I thought the movement might be ending—the next, it began again, with a sweeping fierceness of spirit that took my breath away. And then, with almost quiet insignificance, the second movement was over.

There was a moment of hovering silence, then it began . . . *the perfect expression of what love should be . . . .*

I closed my eyes, letting the melody wrap me in its arms. All the doubts and pain of the past months melted away. The music was *Seriozha* and as long as it played, he was with me . . . holding me, loving me. . . .

Tears streamed down my face as I finally understood what he had been trying to tell me that last night. It was the perfect expression of love . . . our love. And nothing would ever change that. Not distance, separation or death.

A week later, I moved back to Winwood Cottage, welcoming the pain along with the memories. In time, solitude became my friend and companion. I had my painting, long walks by the sea, and when the ache became too unbearable, I had the symphony. Kevin dropped by occasionally, then stopped coming.

In January, Tillamook Community College had an opening for an art instructor, and my application was accepted.

Days and weeks of gray rain and blustering "so'westers"

passed by. Often, I would stand at the seaward edge of Winwood Cottage, watching the troubled seas and wondering if Seriozha were somewhere out on the ocean, thinking of me. And there were nights when the sea was very black, with white waves crashing and pale constellations burning above, when I would see lights far out to sea and wonder if it might be his ship.

In early April, when delicate white trillium first opened their petals along the forest trails, I felt a strange restlessness—an expectancy that at any moment someone might walk in the door and fill my emptiness with warmth. Reality tried to convince me it wasn't possible, but the thought alone was enough to keep a certain spark alive.

Late one afternoon, I returned from class to find a strange car parked in the driveway. My heart leaped, and my pulse was hammering as I ran across the lawn toward the house.

A stocky, gray-haired man in a dark gray suit was leaning against the fence, watching the sea. He turned at the sound of my approach, and I ran into his arms.

"Kolya! Oh, Kolya. . . ."

He kissed my tear-stained cheeks, and I kissed his.

"Dear Cassandra, so often I have thought of you —" He held me away from him and smiled into my face. "Still beautiful," he said, then held me close and let me cry.

I made tea, and we sat at the kitchen table, talking as if no time had separated us. He told me about his work and laughed when I described my classes at the community college.

"With such a lovely instructor for inspiration, I am surprised your students turn in anything besides portraits of you," he said, gallant as ever.

"I have a few students with potential," I told him, "but most of them are more interested in drawing race cars or half-naked battle women."

He laughed again, and I realized how much I had missed hearing the sound. "And what of your own painting?" he asked. "I hope you have continued your work."

"I manage to keep busy."

His hazel eyes were suddenly tender as they gazed into mine.

"Would it give you offense if I asked about the fiance? By this time, I confess I expected you would be married."

I shook my head. "No. Kevin knows I can never marry him. He still doesn't understand why, but. . . ." I glanced down at my cup.

Nikolai leaned forward and put a hand over mine. "Half a moon sheds half a light," he said softly. "Half a love . . . no light at all."

I swallowed hard, holding his hand tightly in mine.

"There is a little time before I must go," he said after a moment. "May I have the pleasure of seeing this house again? And also, any examples of your painting?"

"Of course."

After he had seen the downstairs rooms, I took him up to my studio. Nikolai stood staring at the various paintings in open-mouthed amazement.

Finally, I cleared my throat and said, trying to lighten the moment, "My sister calls this room the *Seriozha Shrine*."

Nikolai smiled. "An apt title, I must agree." He paused to examine an oil portrait of Sergei polishing my grandfather's brass bell. "*Krasivyi* . . . beautiful. . . . My dear, your gift is surpassed only by your love." He looked closer at the title of the painting and tears suddenly filled his eyes. "*Flower of the Winds*. Ah, Kasenya, that is what you are—the lovely compass rose guiding us to safety."

I had thought Nikolai's visit would ease my loneliness. Instead, it made things worse. The pain and emptiness I thought I'd learned to live with became unbearable that evening. Wounds I thought had healed were suddenly fresh and bleeding, and there was nothing to heal them. Not memories or my painting. Not even the symphony.

I hated them all. And for the first time in my life, I hated the house. Grabbing a jacket, I left them all behind and headed down the hillside steps to the sea.

The air was soft, and the sea was calm blue silk as I walked around the point. I stared past the jagged rocks that had once imprisoned a small cabin cruiser, to a deep rose sunset. As the colors changed, fading to mauve and lavender, I tried to hate its beauty. Above me, a thin crescent moon and evening's first star shared the glowing sky. The hatred gradually died, along with the color, leaving only grayness and a deep, heavy ache.

Walking back in subdued grays, I could barely see the rocky walls of the point and a dark shadow moving my way. I stopped short as the shadow formed itself into a man. I blinked and stared as he came steadily toward me, then started to run.

"Seriozha. . . !"

His arms erased the emptiness, and his kiss healed the pain. Looking into his eyes, all the grayness was gone in a moment, swept away in a tide of tears and happiness.

Sea-foam bubbled and hissed around the barnacle-encrusted walls of the point as we walked by. Lifting me in his arms, Sergei carried me down the beach where gulls flirted with the incoming tide. On the dark hillside above us, the lights of Winwood Cottage glowed softly in the dusk.

I smiled into his dark eyes and whispered, "Welcome home, *dushenka.*"

His answer was in Russian, and this time I needed no translation.

— The End —